Lombardo's Law

Lombardo's Law

Ellen Wittlinger

Houghton Mifflin Company
Boston

www.houghtonmifflinbooks.com

Library of Congress Cataloging-in-Publication Data
Wittlinger, Ellen.
Lombardo's law / by Ellen Wittlinger.
p. cm.
Summary: A fifteen-year-old girl and her new thirteen-year-old
male neighbor find their friendship deepening into a romance
as they work on writing and filming a screenplay together.
RNF ISBN 0-395-65969-8 PAP ISBN 0-618-31108-4
[1. Neighborhood—Fiction.] I. Title.
PZ7.W78436Lo 1993 92-28916
[Fic]—dc20 CIP AC

Printed in the United States of America
HAD 10 9 8 7 6 5 4 3 2 1

for my dreamers, Kate and Morgan

Chapter One

It was always my parents' dream to live in New England. It wasn't my dream; that isn't the kind of thing I dream about. For years Mom and Dad had applied for every barely suitable job they heard about within a hundred miles of Boston. The idea was, one of them would get employed, then the other would manage to find something once they got here. I never thought it would really happen. Mom and Dad have always been great dreamers, but none of their dreams ever amounted to much.

I think they were as shocked as I was when Dad was offered the job at Arlington College, about two miles outside the city limits of Boston. He could even teach three courses in his chosen field: Literature and Film. That always cracks me up. I tell him he's got nerve taking money from people to teach Books and Movies. Anyway, they thought they'd died and gone to heaven. They were not terribly concerned that this place was not *my* idea of heaven.

I don't know what the big deal is about New England. I mean, O.K., it's pretty, sort of, and old, but the way people talk about it, you'd think it was the only place in the country where autumn leaves change colors. All fall everybody kept pointing up to regular old maple trees and saying, "Have you ever seen anything like *this?*" As though we were from Mars. When I told kids I was from Iowa, they'd get it mixed up with Ohio or Idaho, and when I tried to straighten them out on their lousy geography, they'd just laugh and flip their hands in the air, like who could possibly care about all those silly vowel-states anyway? After all, they weren't in *New England.*

Don't get me wrong. It's not that I miss Iowa all that much. Although there's plenty about it that's just as pretty as Massachusetts. But I didn't leave any broken hearts behind when I moved, if you know what I mean. Most of the boys in my class were pretty juvenile, and the two or three that weren't juvenile were just plain conceited. I had a few girlfriends, but they were mostly friends with each other and just nice enough to let me hang around with them when I wanted to, which wasn't all that often.

I like to be by myself. I actually prefer it. Not just sitting around my room moping or anything. I do stuff. Like in Iowa we lived right near the University and there was always a movie going on somewhere, either a foreign film or a documentary at the school, or the usual stuff at the theater in town. Dad talked Mom into letting me go by myself to matinees, which is my favorite way to see movies. Otherwise you keep thinking about whether the person you're seeing the movie with likes it or not. If they're groaning all through it, or laughing hysterically, it's hard to have your own pure reaction. If you like the person and they like the movie, you sort of feel like liking it too, even if you don't really. And vice versa if you *don't* like the person. And if the person ends up *talking* through the whole movie I end up hating *them*.

I also do a lot of reading and writing. I read anything, but I love Brock Cole and Anne Tyler and J. D. Salinger because all their characters are regular weirdos, like me. I mean, you wouldn't notice them or anything, but they're strange and cool, even though people don't know it. Not that I think I'm cool. I'm not. The older I get the more I have to remind myself of how that doesn't matter.

I write all the time too — poetry, plays, stories — whatever enters my brain — but I didn't plan to show anybody until I was as good as J.D. himself. Sometimes plans change.

I couldn't say what I look like really. When I look in the mirror, I know it's the same old me, but whether I'm good-looking or not is just too hard to figure out. My mother says I could do more with what I've got, but she's not really into dolling up either. I'm on the tall side, which I like, but my hair is that unfortunate color called "dirty blonde." It's short and straight and I usually forget to get it cut until I can barely see out from under the bangs.

I'm fifteen, a mere year from my driver's license, if only I lived in a normal place. Only a person with suicidal tendencies would choose to get behind a wheel in old Beantown. Actually, we live in Allerton, a suburb of Boston, and not such a bad place, even though everyone I meet thinks Midwesterners are aliens.

These two girls used to sit with me at lunch and constantly ask me what I liked best about living in New England, and beg me to admit how superior it is to Iowa. I got tired of them and moved to the table with kids who read while they eat. No talking allowed.

The best thing about the place we live is I can get on a bus and be in Cambridge in fifteen minutes, which is much cooler than Boston and full of movie theaters. Only my dad says it's not safe to go alone in the city. He goes with me sometimes, and he's very quiet, but I've missed some great films when he was too busy to go. So I put my mind to finding a cohort when school started again, not even a friend, just another slightly off-center movie lover to go into Cambridge with.

And then *they* moved in, right across the street, in the house that should have been mine.

Chapter Two

I loved that house the moment I saw it. The realtor had brought us to look at the place across the street, the one my parents eventually bought, which is just a regular house with three bedrooms and a front porch. But when I saw that the house across the street had a For Sale sign too, I began to beg shamelessly.

"I'll contribute my baby-sitting money to the down payment! I'll cut the grass every week! I'll practice the piano half an hour every day!" I was obviously getting desperate. "I'll even" — I shuddered — "empty the cat box without being told!"

But Dad the dreamer had turned practical on me. "It's much too big, Justine. We don't need a palace, nor can we afford one."

"It's empty. I can show it to you just for fun, if you like," the realtor said. I wondered if she'd ever seen a whining kid talk her parents into buying a house they didn't want. Then she qualified: "The asking price is quite a bit more than your ballpark, though. And it needs some work done besides."

Dad had no interest, but I could tell by looking at Mom that she'd entered the world of imagination. She had a wistful look on her face, and I would have bet money she was seeing a ten-foot lit-up Christmas tree standing inside that big bay window in the living room.

"It wouldn't hurt to just *look* at it, Oliver. It's a magnificent house."

So we took a look, just for fun, as Dad kept reminding us. The house was a Victorian, Mom said, and had about fifteen rooms with big windows down to the floor and porches sticking out all over the place. Then I found *my* room — big and light like all the others, but two of the big windows turned out to be doors, and when you opened them there was a private balcony just for that room. It faced the back yard, so that when the trees were all leaved out you could sit there and be invisible from the street or any other house. A secret place!

"For instance," the realtor continued, "these porch railings should be replaced, and you'd need to repaint in a few years if you want to keep your shingles in shape."

"No, thanks," Dad said, "these aren't the shingles for us. Could we go back across the street a moment? I'd like to take another look at the furnace."

I knew that when Dad started talking furnaces, the dream was dead. So instead of moving into the

Palace, as I had begun to think of the house, we moved close enough to it for me to be constantly reminded of what I was missing.

The Palace stood there, lovely and lonely, for a year. In the fall some kid came and raked leaves, and in the spring he came back to cut the grass. It seemed only right that no one else should be allowed to move into my dream house.

But then, right at the end of the summer, a huge moving van pulled up one morning, towing a Volvo station wagon behind it, and people began unloading piles of big, heavy furniture, just the kind of stuff you'd expect to see in a house like that. I'll tell you, I was depressed.

Not Mom. She was getting dressed for her job as a children's librarian — a job she loves because you don't have to wear high heels and you can sing "I'm a Little Teapot" and read ghost stories and organize pet shows all day long — but she kept running back to the window and giving me the New Neighbors Update.

"Ooh, they've got one of those enormous TVs. I think I'd be afraid to turn it on — Oh, Justine, you should see the beautiful armoire that just went inside. And a canopy bed — Racks and racks of clothing are coming out of that truck. Who could even wear all those clothes? Maybe they have a lot of children — Justine, maybe they'll need a baby-sitter!"

Great, I thought. I can go to the Palace as hired

help. I figured they'd probably have about six little brats, all spoiled rotten.

"Oh, look, this must be the family!" Mom called out on one of her inspection tours past the window. "Goodness. A Volvo and a Mercedes." She sighed. "Well, I guess we knew they'd be rich. But maybe we'll like them anyway!" she said cheerfully.

I like that about my Mom: she knows how the world is likely to work, but she's optimistic anyway. I couldn't resist a peek at the lucky new home owners. A middle-aged man jumped out of the Mercedes and slammed the door, then strode over to one of the moving men to give him what looked like a large piece of his mind. Then a woman got out slowly and arched her back as though it was tired. She turned around to talk to whoever was still sitting inside. Then she closed the car door and went into the house.

After a minute both back doors of the car flew open. A girl got out on one side and a boy on the other, and they were fighting.

"They might be about your age, Justine, don't you think? Especially the girl. Wouldn't it be nice to have a friend living so close by?"

With the window open I could hear the shouting, but I couldn't make out what the fight was about. I was pretty sure the girl called the boy "Pea-brain."

"Just because she's my age, which we don't even know yet, doesn't mean she'll be my friend,

Mother." She has a thing about how I don't have enough friends, which is true, but not a national disaster.

Mom was in La-La-Land already. "When I was a girl, Susan Marshall lived across the street and we were like twins, everybody always said. We were together from morning till night. We told each other everything. When she moved away during our junior year in high school it was the saddest thing that ever happened to either one of us."

I'd heard the Saint Susan stories plenty of times already, so I didn't encourage her with any questions.

"Well, I'm going to introduce myself before I leave for work. Come with me," she demanded. "It's only polite."

So five minutes later we were standing in the kitchen of the Palace, surrounded by cardboard boxes marked "Crystal" and "Wedgwood," shaking hands with strangers. The mother seemed like a person with a bad headache. She leaned against the sink and hardly moved any part of her velour-covered body. But she was nice to Mom and offered her a cup of tea, which Mom refused.

Then there was this boy who was obviously young, at most twelve or thirteen; a kid with an attitude problem is the way he looked to me. He scowled through the introductions and then stomped off upstairs. After he left, I couldn't even remember what he'd looked like, probably because it was hard to see some plain-looking kid when you were standing in the same room with *her*.

Her name was Heather, Heather Lombardo, and she was gorgeous. She had that thick kind of black hair that just tumbles across your shoulders, and dark olive skin with dark, dark eyes. On the small side, but with the kind of shape boys walk into walls while they're looking at it. I could already see a line of sophomore nincompoops banging each other into lockers and shoving each other up and down the hallway to get her attention. Because, like me, she was fifteen, a sophomore this fall at Allerton High School. Unlike me, she would never be invisible.

"You'll have to come to dinner once you've settled in," Mom was saying earnestly.

"Oh, don't go to any trouble," Mrs. Lombardo whispered. Her pupils started racing around her eyes.

"Don't be silly. We're still newcomers ourselves. It'll be fun to get together." Sometimes Mom's enthusiasm is blind.

It looked to me like Mrs. Lombardo's idea of fun might not be dinner with the neighbors. But she smiled a little. "Well, thank you. We'll see."

When Mom suggested Heather ride to school with us the first morning, I really thought she'd crossed over the invisible line between Midwestern good will and down-home pushiness. I backed toward the door to separate myself from this plan, but Heather said, "Oh, great!" like she meant it. Still, something told me the days of Heather Lombardo riding to school in Jean and Oliver Trainor's ancient Dodge would be limited.

Chapter Three

It seemed that in some further conversation with Mrs. Lombardo, my dear mother expanded her offer of a ride to school to include Heather's younger brother, Mike, an eighth grader at the junior high.

"Couldn't he take the bus?" I complained.

"Why should he, if I'm driving you girls anyway? The junior high is only a few blocks from the high school."

"I know that, Mother, but the thing is . . ." What exactly was the thing? "I mean, I doubt that somebody like Heather enjoys riding around with her little brother in the car."

"Justine, I don't know what you're talking about." But from the look she was giving me, I suspected she had a clue.

"You're the one who thinks I should be best buddies with the kid across the street. I'm just telling you she won't like hanging around with her brother."

"Well, maybe you should *all* just take the bus then," Mom said pointedly. She had me there. It was out of her way to drop me off at school every morning before she went to work, but I'd begged her. I'd do anything to avoid that stupid bus. It was packed with kids from the junior high. They threw books and spitballs and doughnuts at each other. They tripped you when you got on, stole the hat off your head, and fell in your lap when the bus lurched. Especially the eighth-grade boys. They acted as though their brains had been sucked out of their heads, like Hungarian Easter eggs.

And now my mother had invited one into the *car* with us. I just hoped when he made some friends among the other juvenile delinquents, he'd prefer to ride the bus.

The first day of school Heather came skipping out of the house wearing black spandex bike shorts and a painted T-shirt that looked like silk. Her hair was tied back with a loose pink scarf in a way that made it seem nothing could really hold that wild, shiny stuff back. She had a pretty thick paint job on her face and stared at me in mock panic.

"You're not going to sit in front, are you? And leave me alone in back with the cretin?"

I smiled uncertainly and then turned to my mom with a little I-told-you-so glare. "Your brother won't mind riding up front with my mom?"

"Who cares? He can walk if he doesn't like it."

"Actually there's a bus . . ." I began, after seating myself in the rear, but Heather had pulled out her schedule and was onto other things.

"Who's this Amperson guy? Is he hard? I didn't want to take geometry anyway, but my dad is making me."

"Oh, Mr. Amperson's nice," I assured her. "You'll like him."

"I doubt it." She tossed her hair forward so I couldn't see her scowling face for a minute. "My old school was, like, great. We could smoke during study halls and go out for a hamburger at lunchtime if we didn't want to eat the slop they served in the cafeteria. But I hear this place is a prison."

"Umm." I'd never thought of it that way, but then I had no trouble getting through the day without a cigarette or a hamburger. "Where did you live before this?"

She sighed heavily. "Well, Connecticut just before, and then New Mexico before that, a little time in California, Florida . . . that's all I remember."

"Your family moves around a lot," I said, stating the obvious. "We moved here last year from Iowa."

Heather looked at me without comprehension. "My mother says we're not moving again; she's had it with moving. Can you believe *this* is the place she decides to put her foot down? Noplace, Massachusetts."

"What does your father do, Heather?" Mom

14

asked, trying to sound interested but not down-right nosy.

"I don't know. He, like, buys businesses and runs them for a while, and then he sells them again when he gets bored."

I didn't notice Mike getting in the car until the front door closed quietly. Mom did the usual polite-mother routine on him and he answered her, but then he was silent for the rest of the ride.

Heather asked for my opinion on all her teach-ers, though she didn't seem to believe that any teacher could be worth much. We had only English class together, and my confession that I'd actually been looking forward to school so I could be in Ms. Dowling's class left her open-mouthed with either disbelief or disgust, I wasn't sure which.

I had begun to suspect that this was not going to be a friendship forged by the gods by the time we arrived at the high school. I was probably not going to develop a great interest in matching my nail pol-ish to my eye shadow, and I suspected Heather would not be interested in borrowing my ragged copy of Edith Hamilton's *Greek Mythology*.

I hopped out on my side of the car and waved goodbye to Mom, then turned to wait for Heather. But she was taking her time. She reminded me of a bride getting out of a limousine, careful not to muss her outfit and certain that everyone is snap-ping her picture.

I've always enjoyed my invisibility, even though

lately I regret being such a total loner. I like being quiet and noticing things and having my own thoughts. I just wish I knew how to talk to a boy when I had the chance, or even had a girlfriend to talk to about him. But standing there next to Heather, watching the heads swivel, the eyes open a little wider, the smiles and giggles and whispers all around us, I wanted to disappear. Being the center of attention makes me dizzy.

Mom drove off with the eighth grader and left us standing there, Beauty and the Beast. Heather threw a big smile in my direction while her eyes gazed over my shoulder at her new subjects. "So, show me around!" she ordered.

Chapter Four

By noon at least six kids, two of whom absolutely never speak to me otherwise, had stopped to ask me about "the new girl." Who was she, were we good friends, did she have a boyfriend, which classes was she in? Because I had pitifully few answers to their questions, most of them gave up pretty quickly.

Only one, this guy Jackson Demuth, kept it up. "You got out of a car with her this morning, didn't you? All I'm asking is, is she taken already? Because I don't feel like wasting my time if she is, okay? I mean, she's a piece of work, all right, but I'm not desperate."

Now normally a guy with as little brain and as much self-adoration as Jackson Demuth does not bother with me, and I thank my lucky stars. But Jackson and I had been assigned as lab partners in science last year and he had come to have a grudging respect for and total misunderstanding of my intellect. He thought I was "one of those geniuses" who never have to study, when in fact, there are a number of subjects that I actually enjoy studying, and several others that I get good grades in anyway because I'm just in the habit of learning.

The problem with Jackson Demuth is that he's Godawful gorgeous. Even as every word coming out of his mouth was grating on my nerves, he'd accidentally rub his smooth muscled arm against mine, reaching for a test tube or something, and my stomach would drop to my feet. I'd mean to make a sarcastic comment about his inability to understand osmosis, but when I glanced into his dark, sunken eyes, my tongue would stumble over my teeth while a guttural whisper escaped my throat. It was downright humiliating, although I assumed he was so used to feminine idiocy in his presence that I seemed perfectly normal to him.

Even having a two-minute conversation with him in the cafeteria could raise my standing in Allerton High social circles, not to mention my blood pressure. "Really, Jackson, I don't know. She lives across the street from me, but she just moved in last week. I haven't seen any guys around." I felt the insipid grin spread across my face as I tried not to fall into his eyes.

"Well, were you looking?" he demanded, running his hand through his black hair, frustrated with me.

"No! I don't stare out the window to see who's visiting the neighbors."

"Well, maybe you ought to."

"Why?"

"Wouldn't hurt ya." He grinned. I choked.

"What wouldn't hurt me?"

"Take a few pointers from her. Now don't get mad, Genius, I'm just telling you for your own good. You're not bad-looking, you know."

Thus endeth my conversation with Jackson Demuth. As he swiveled off across the cafeteria, I tried to convince myself I was furious with him. The arrogant snot! Who did he think he was? Meanwhile the other half of my brain kept singing, "Jackson Demuth thinks I'm not bad-looking!"

By the time I walked home from school, happily alone, I had managed to divert my anger onto Heather. Why had this complication entered my life? Who needed some jazzy neighbor around to make me feel nerdy?

I placed a call to the library as I always did as soon as I got home.

"Hi, I'm home. See you later."

"Wait!" Mom caught me before I signed off. "Did you help Heather around at school? Did you walk home with her?"

"No and no. Heather doesn't need any help. Heather probably had several athletic teams waiting to walk her home."

"Oh, honey, are you sure you've given her a fair chance? I know she doesn't *seem* exactly like your type . . ."

"Mom, I'm sorry, but Heather Lombardo is no Susan Marshall. We are not, I repeat *not*, going to be best friends."

"Okay." Mom sighed. "I'm not pushing you. What are your plans for the afternoon?"

"Read, I guess."

"Justine, it's a beautiful day. Do me a favor and get outside a little. Get some air."

I didn't bother to argue that I'd just walked a mile and a half on this beautiful day. I was agreeable, and then I could hang up.

There was one old, frosty Fudgsicle left in the freezer and I dug it out. I thought I'd just sit on the front porch and read, so as to fulfill my air-getting promise, but as I banged out the squeaky screen door, the two people walking down the sidewalk turned and looked up at me. Jackson Demuth and Heather Lombardo, each of them giddy with happiness at having found someone as stunning as themselves to latch on to.

"Hi, Justine!" Heather sang out, giving my name four or five syllables. "I wondered where you'd sneaked off to!"

Jackson gave me his famous half-smile-half-smirk, but I was oddly unmoved.

"You two met." What else was there to say? How

20

could I deign to comment on the most obviously perfect match in the history of Allerton High School?

"We're going to go study," Heather announced seriously.

"Right!" Jackson laughed heartily.

"Jackson, we *are!*" Heather insisted prettily, tossing her hair in his face and poking an elbow into his solid chest.

Jackson tried to grab her around the waist, but she gave a little scream and ran across the street, Popeye in hot pursuit. I watched until they ran in the front door of the Palace. I didn't want to watch, but somehow I couldn't stop myself. I just kept standing there looking even though they'd gone inside.

Then from the side of our house came this voice, and I just about fell over the porch railing in surprise. It said, "You don't like her either, do you?"

Chapter Five

A boy who looked vaguely familiar came out from behind our bushes, backpack on his back, his hand in a bag of potato chips.

"I could tell this morning in the car you wouldn't like her. Believe me, I'm not accusing you. It's to your credit."

"You're her brother!"

"Unfortunately, yes." He held out the potato chip bag, but I shook my head.

"Why were you hiding in our bushes?"

"I wasn't exactly hiding. Mind if I sit down on your steps a minute? I don't feel like facing the Stupids yet."

"I guess not." I realized I'd been letting the Fudgsicle drip down all over my hand. In confusion I sat down on the step above Heather's brother.

"I'm sorry, I forgot your name."

"As usual. Reach into my backpack — I've got some paper towels. You're covered with chocolate."

This was getting downright embarrassing. An eighth-grade boy telling me to clean myself up. What next? I threw the remains of the ice cream bar into the bushes and sat down to peer hesitantly into his backpack.

"Mike. My name is Mike. Instantly forgettable. Unlike Heather. What a breathless little name that is. My parents must have reached deep into the well of dumbness to come up with it."

"So why were you not-exactly-hiding in our bushes?"

"Well, I was just taking my time walking home from school. I was looking at things, like seeing where we live. I mean, what this place is all about, who lives here and everything. I stopped down the block to talk to two little kids who were trying to fly a kite. It was a great kite, with a big monster face on it."

"Flying a kite today? There's not a breath of air moving."

"I know. That's what was so great. They couldn't get this thing to go up at all, and I explained to them that you needed a good wind to get a kite in the air. They kept saying, 'We know,' but then they'd keep on trying to get the thing up. Or that's what I thought. So finally they got tired of me interrupting them with my expertise and they said, 'We're not trying to *fly* the kite, we're just *pulling* it.' And they were. I mean, I kept thinking they wanted to get it in the air, because that's what I've always done with a kite, but here these kids had already adapted to the problem of no wind and they were having a good time anyway. I loved that."

This kid was obviously not your run-of-the-mill eighth grader. What Heather had in looks, he had in oddness. But he was funny. I didn't even mind sitting right out in public with him.

"So, what does all this have to do with our bushes?"

"Simple. While I was dawdling, I heard He-Man and She-Ra coming. I had to make a quick getaway and I didn't want to go home and have to listen to them oohing and aahing over each other, so your bushes were the first available cover I came to."

"I see. Well, feel free to escape to our bushes whenever you need to."

"Thanks. You still didn't answer my question."

I hadn't forgotten it. "Do I like your sister?"

"Do you?"

"I've only spoken to her for about ten minutes in my life."

"You can tell about somebody in ten minutes."

I gave him my annoyed look. "Are you always so persistent?"

"Yeah," he said, and smiled. Just for a minute, he looked very cute, and I was shocked that I could think that way about such a kid, a boy three inches shorter than me! I mean, he was thirteen!

"Actually," he continued, "you don't even have to answer me, because I know already."

"What do you know, Genius?" I countered, giving him my own nickname.

"I know you couldn't like Heather. Because you're the kind of person I could like. And no one I could like could possibly like my sister. Lombardo's Law." He stood and picked up his backpack. "Gotta go. See you around, huh?"

"Guess so," I answered without getting up. I didn't want him to think I'd get right up and leave just because he was going. Like I had something else important to do on the front porch steps.

I watched him cross the street and go inside, just a plain-looking kid, really, although once you'd talked to him, he certainly didn't seem so ordinary anymore.

And what did he mean, he *could* like me? Could if he wanted to? Could if he was older? Or had I passed my ten-minute trial and he liked me already? And what did *that* mean, a thirteen-year-old boy liking a fifteen-year-old girl? He was one weird kid.

Chapter Six

The next morning in the car Heather couldn't shut up about Jackson Demuth. "He is so adorable with those big brown eyes. I just love that type, don't you? You know he's sixteen already? He's getting his driver's license this week!"

"Don't you have to know how to read and write to take the driver's test?" Mike asked innocently from the front seat. I suppressed a smile.

Heather was so good at ignoring her brother, you could almost believe she hadn't heard him. "Maybe we can double-date sometime, Justine. Who are you going out with?"

Obviously it took Heather longer than ten minutes to sum up a new acquaintance. "Well, actually, I'm not dating anyone. I don't really . . . date."

Heather shot me a look of horror, then whispered, "You mean your mother doesn't let you?"

"I mean, the subject has never come up."

I wasn't sure whether Heather really understood this confession. She searched my face for additional clues, then gave me a noncommittal "Oh" in response.

"Heather thinks it's strange if people aren't going steady by the fourth grade," Mike put in from the front seat.

"This is the time in your lives when you should be making lots of friends, and doing things with groups of kids." Poor Mom just couldn't adjust to my lack of intimate associates. She couldn't believe I wasn't miserable spending so much time alone. All of a sudden I felt really angry that Heather wasn't Susan Marshall. It would have solved problems for all of us.

"Oh, I agree!" Heather chimed in. "I love big parties. And I don't go steady with one person for a long time. I like to switch around. Although" — she giggled — "I'll make an exception for Jackson."

I was beginning to think this morning ride situation just might be intolerable.

Things were back to normal in school, though. Nobody asked me about Heather; I suppose enough other people had talked to her by now that I was no longer the only expert on the subject. At lunchtime I sat with the two Jennifers, the readers, as usual. Jennifer Holtz and Jennifer Wolodny. We just said "hi" to each other and then buried ourselves in our books for the rest of the period.

Heather walked into English class with two very popular girls. They were laughing about something as they passed my desk, and Heather did not look over at me, or stop to chat, as she had the day before. It was nothing short of a relief to think that our days of chumhood might already be over.

Walking home, I found myself slowing down and looking around, using Mike's method of "seeing" my relatively new hometown. It's a pretty place, in an ordinary kind of way. I mean, there are white churches with big steeples, just the way you're supposed to have in New England, and a small lake and several parks. But there's also this kind of crummy downtown part with a Wendy's and a Pizza Pan and a couple of chintzy clothing stores. The five-and-ten closed down before we moved here, but the sign is still up and the windows are soaped over.

I was actually standing outside this store, kind of trying to see inside through the soap, when I heard a commotion across the street. Eighth-grade boys, of course. Male hormones are truly revolting those first few years.

There was a group of three or four boys who seemed to be following another boy, taunting him. "What a brown-nose. Ooh, he's smart; he's from Connecticut!" In falsetto, they imitated him: "I've already read that book, Mrs. Smithwick! Could I choose a different Newbery book? Pick the longest, hardest book you can think of, Mrs. Smithwick; I'll read that!" They laughed uproariously.

Suddenly the boy in front swung around with a furious look on his face, his arms held in front of him, his hands in fists, as though he would take them all on. It was Mike.

"You think it's so damn cool to be dumb?" he yelled, then punched his fists out into the air, far from the boys in front of him, as though he was just practicing for a fight.

The boys stopped, surprised for a moment, then one of them stepped up to Mike and punched him in the stomach. "Is this what you're asking me for? Is this what you want?" Mike doubled over, and the boys laughed again, then pushed him aside and walked on.

I couldn't decide what I should do. What if he was hurt? Should I go over and see if I could help him? I knew he'd be embarrassed that I saw the whole thing. As I stood there on the corner, trying to decide, Mike straightened up and looked right at me. His eyes focused and glared. Then he turned and ran. By the time I had crossed the street he was out of sight.

The following morning when Heather trooped out to our car in yet another stunning outfit, she announced, "My idiot brother isn't riding with us anymore, thank God. He left half an hour ago. He says he'd rather walk."

I sank back into the seat, surprised at my disappointment, and listened halfheartedly as Heather discussed the social events she might choose to attend during the coming weekend.

Chapter Seven

Heather called Sunday evening to say she would be riding to school with Jackson from now on. "We're kind of going steady." She giggled. "But tell your mom thanks a lot anyway. She is just so super!"

"Heather says you're so super," I reported. "But not quite as super as Jackson Demuth."

Mom shook her head. "How can they be going steady after one week? You kids don't even get to know each other before you pair off these days."

"Don't include me in this complaint! I don't pair off at all."

Mom smiled sadly. "I didn't mean you. You have much too much sense to do anything so impulsive."

Somehow this didn't strike me as a compliment. "Don't give me credit for something I can't even help. Do you think I'm holding all these boys at bay?" I pantomimed holding off the hordes. "No, no, Matt, I couldn't possibly ride in your car. Oh, Steve, do you think I'm so impulsive as to go on a date with you? Ha, ha, Jason, I have too much sense to speak to you in the hall between classes."

Now Mom actually closed her book; we were going to talk. "Justine, I don't quite understand. On the one hand, you act as though you're perfectly happy being alone, reading, writing, thinking. You convince me you don't need a lot of close friendships. But then you say something like this and I think I was wrong not to push you to meet people. I know it's not easy. I'm actually . . . somewhat lonely here myself."

I knew this was true. Mom had had a bunch of women friends in Iowa, some she'd known since college. And although nobody ever measured up to old Susan Marshall, she spent a good deal of time talking things over with her friends. Should she have another child? Should she go back to work? Should we move to the East Coast?

When we first got here, Mom was so thrilled to be in a History Hot Spot that all she cared about was dragging us around to visit all the famous places: the Old North Church, the Freedom Trail, the U.S.S. *Constitution*. But now that we were more like citizens than vacationers, I suspected she was a little disappointed.

"Of course it's not so important to Dad," she continued. "He's got his colleagues at work. The only

31

other stimulation he requires is a movie theater or a good bookstore, and there are plenty of those around. I always think you're just like Dad, but maybe I'm wrong."

"Those things are important to me. I *am* like Dad," I said, still pouting a little.

"But you're fifteen years old. And you *should* have friends. You've isolated yourself here, Justine."

"It's not just here, Mom. I was isolated in Iowa too."

"But I don't know why. You're bright and attractive. A little shy, maybe . . ."

"I'm not shy! People always say people are shy if they don't want to just jabber about any dumb subject that comes up!"

"Okay, you're not shy. But you're lonely, aren't you?"

"Not too much. Once in a while. I'd like to have a good friend, but all the girls want to talk about is boys. And the boys are too stupid for words."

"What about those two girls you eat lunch with?"

"They're shy."

Mom sighed. "Well, I don't know what advice to give you, Justine. I'm sure there are other kids like you, intelligent and interested in the world, but it may take some work to figure out who they are. I have a feeling you're one of those people who blossom in college."

32

"That's three years from now! I don't want to be dormant for three more years!" I yelled, not sure just which side I was arguing. I stomped upstairs and slammed the door to my room, just to make some noise, to prove I was a real person, not some timid plant waiting around to bloom.

Chapter Eight

I decided to make an effort. I sat down at the table with the two Jennifers and gave them both a big smile.

"What are you reading?" Funny it had never occurred to me to ask them before. They both looked surprised.

"The new Stephen King," Jennifer Holtz said. "I read everything he writes. He's awesome."

Not a satisfactory answer. I hate horror books and horror movies and even ghost stories. I turned to the other Jennifer. Definitely the quieter of the two, she had her arm over her book as though she didn't want me to see it.

"You wouldn't like it," she said and turned away.

"I just wondered what it was. It's not like I plan to read it."

She sighed. "It's poetry, okay?"

"Really? You read poetry?"

She didn't answer.

"Well, who? Like Robert Frost?" I liked Frost myself.

"No, not like Robert Frost," she said with a certain note of disdain in her voice.

"Well, who then?" I was amazed to realize she assumed she was smarter than I was.

"If you must know, I'm reading Wallace Stevens."

"I've heard of him."

"Have you read him?" she said sort of hopefully.

"No. But I've read Robert Lowell."

"You have? I love Robert Lowell! *Life Studies!*" Her cheeks got all rosy.

"Yeah, that's what I read. It was good. I liked all his weird relatives. My mom is a librarian, so she's always bringing books home. I read whatever is lying around."

"How discriminating. Have you read Elizabeth Bishop or Sylvia Plath?"

"No. I guess Lowell and Robert Frost are about as far as I've gotten in poetry."

She looked me over suspiciously, as though trying to decide if I was worth the money she was about to spend. Finally she mumbled, "I could lend them to you, if you like."

"Sure. I'll read anything."

I'm not sure that was the response she was hoping for, but she smiled weakly before turning back to Wallace Stevens. I didn't have the feeling I'd

cemented a lifelong friendship with Jennifer Wolodny here at the lunch table, but at least I'd had
an interesting conversation with someone about
something other than the opposite sex.

I was halfway home that afternoon, without an
umbrella, when the sun disappeared. I hadn't lived
in Iowa for fourteen years without knowing when
a thunderstorm is coming, but there wasn't much
to do. I walked a little faster, but the rain came up
all of a sudden. By the time I'd run half a block to
the shelter of the Pizza Pan doorway, I was soaked.
No sooner had I flattened myself against the door
than a boy came racing in and banged into me.

"Watch it!" I said, not too thrilled to be soaking
wet and still fifteen minutes from home.

"Hi," the kid said, and then I saw it was Mike,
my punched-in-the-stomach neighbor.

"Oh, hey! Haven't seen you in a while."

"Yeah." He smiled this big goofy smile he had.
"You look as good as I do." His hair was mashed
to his forehead and dripping down his face. Great.
But he laughed, so it didn't seem like any tragedy.

"You know what?" Mike said. "Maybe my mom
could come pick us up, unless she's got a migraine
or something. It's worth a try."

So we went into the Pizza Pan and he called
home. But apparently his mother *was* having a
headache. I stood a little bit away so it didn't seem
like I was eavesdropping, but I heard it all anyway.

"It's pouring out! We'll get soaked! No, her

mother is at work. Well, can't you take another pill? Okay, okay. Goodbye."

"Headache?" I asked sympathetically.

"Yeah, she's always got a headache. She doesn't like driving, either. She said we should just stay here until it stops."

"We don't have much choice."

"Do you want to eat something? They probably won't let us hang around if we don't."

I called my mother too, so she wouldn't freak out. If she doesn't hear from me by three-thirty every day, she can barely restrain herself from dialing 911.

"We're going to have a piece of pizza and wait it out. It's probably just a local storm."

"You're with Mike? From across the street? How did you happen to meet him?"

"We just both ran in here to get out of the rain." I was conscious of the fact that Mike couldn't help hearing everything I said.

"Well, I guess that's good. You don't really know him, do you?"

I tried to keep my voice low and indistinct. "He rode to school with us, remember?"

"I know, but you didn't speak to him. He's at the Junior High, isn't he?"

"Yes." I wanted to say, this isn't a date, Mother, but I couldn't very well say that with Mike sitting right there.

"Well, okay. If it keeps raining, I'll leave work

early and come and get you. You're all right, aren't you?"

"Why wouldn't I be?"

"Oh, I don't know. You're wet and everything . . ."

"It's seventy-five degrees outside. I'm not likely to get pneumonia or polio or anything."

"Don't be smart. That's not what I meant."

"Goodbye, Mom. I'll call you when I get home." I turned around to see that Mike had already gotten us each a piece of pepperoni pizza and a Coke.

"Is this okay?"

"Great."

"Your mom thinks you're going to die of wetness?"

I shook my head. "Mothers."

"Yeah. Yours seems okay, though. At least she's not a loony tunes. Mine thinks she's sick all the time. She doesn't even want to leave the house."

It occurred to me then that I hadn't seen Mrs. Lombardo since the day the family moved in two weeks before. And it also occurred to me, as the door to the Pizza Pan kept opening and closing, that it might look to anybody coming in as if Mike and I actually *were* on a date. A quick glance around assured me that I didn't know any of the kids there. Not that it mattered what anybody thought, I told myself. He's my neighbor. Can't I eat pizza with my neighbor?

"Don't want your friends to see you with an eighth grader, huh?"

38

I was stricken dumb.

"I don't blame you. I might think it was embarrassing to be seen with an older girl, too, except I don't have any friends here, so it doesn't matter."

"I wasn't thinking that."

"Yes you were."

I really didn't mind this kid. He was funny.

"Okay, I was. But then I remembered I don't have any friends either."

"Oh, that slipped your mind?"

"Momentarily. Now you tell me something. How come you ran away so fast last week after that kid hit you?"

Mike got quiet and kind of white in the face. He licked his lips, but he didn't say anything. I was sorry I'd mentioned it.

"I mean, I just wondered what was going on. Did he hurt you?"

"No, it feels really good to get punched like that."

"You know what I mean."

"Look, it's no big deal. This always happens when you move to a new place. Eventually I'll probably meet somebody like me and it'll be fine. But you know how guys this age are. Macho. Threatened by anybody who has two consecutive thoughts."

"Did you have a good friend in Connecticut?"

"Connecticut wasn't so great. But we didn't stay there too long. A year or so. Before that was New Mexico. I was really happy in New Mexico — this little sagebrush town. We lived there for three years; I can hardly remember before that, California or Florida."

"What did you do in New Mexico? Ride horses?"

He laughed. "Not exactly. I had this friend Harry — the supreme nerd. Great kid. His dad had a tremendous collection of old movies on video, really classic stuff, and Harry and I would come home after school and plug in a movie. Sometimes we'd watch the same one over and over until we knew all the dialogue. We could do Sherlock Holmes and Dr. Watson in *The Hound of the Baskervilles* word for word. That's where I learned to love movies. Which was good, because it's the only thing that kept me alive in Connecticut."

I was staring at Mike as though he'd just told me a great whopper of a lie.

"What's the matter?"

"Nothing. You love movies?"

"Movies are my one and only love. Which is one good thing about living here. I can bop into Cambridge on the bus and see something great almost any day."

"Your parents let you go into Cambridge alone?"

"My parents don't really care much what I do. Or Heather either, for that matter. Dad is very busy with work and Mom is 'sick' all the time. It suits me. Nobody looks over my shoulder."

"You are so lucky!" A tinge of outrage colored

my voice. "I would die to be able to go to the movies in Cambridge, but my parents won't let me go alone. When we lived in Iowa I went all the time, but here they're afraid of everything."

"Could you go with me?"

I considered. Go with Mike. They might allow it. But then I'd be with Mike, not on a date, of course, but out with him on what would *look* like a date to anyone else. But who was this anyone else I was so worried about? It was nobody else's business who I hung around with. "Maybe they'd let me. I don't know."

"But you might not want to go with me."

"No, it's not that. It's just . . . actually I really like to go to movies alone, to get my pure reaction. I know it sounds silly."

Now it was Mike's turn to be surprised. "Me too! I love to go alone! I mean watching with Harry was okay, but even he would talk out loud sometimes and wreck everything. Even if I like the movie, but the other person is liking it too *much*, it bugs me."

"I never talk out loud during a movie. Never."

"Me either. It's a sin. There's a double bill Hitchcock at the Brattle on Saturday."

"Is it *The Lady Vanishes?*"

"And *Rear Window*."

"I'm dead! I'm in heaven! Let's go!"

Mike grinned and finished off his pizza bones and then mine.

Chapter Nine

"You're going to the movies with Mike?" My mother looked downright astonished. "But he's quite a bit younger than you, isn't he?"

"So what? We're going to the movies, not getting married. It isn't even a date."

"I guess I just can't imagine what the two of you have in common. I mean, he seems nice enough . . ."

"Mom, you don't even know him. Actually, I think we have quite a bit in common. For instance, we both love movies, old movies, foreign movies, weird movies. I've been here a year and I haven't found anybody else who wants to go to the movies with me. Let's don't make a big deal out of this, okay?"

"I'm not making a big deal out of it, it's just . . ."

"You're the one who was so desperate for me to make friends with the people across the street, just like you and Susan Marshall."

"I was not desperate. And I thought you'd make friends with the *girl,* not the boy."

"Are you saying girls and boys can't be friends?"

"No, but . . ."

"Don't you have friends who are younger than you? Don't you have male friends? You told me you and Daddy were friends for a long time before you fell in love. You always say in the sixties nobody went on dates — you all just hung out together and were friends."

"Well, that's true, but . . ." She stopped and laughed. "Justine, I hate it when you quote my good advice back to me when I've forgotten I ever gave it to you. You're right, I'm making a big deal out of nothing. Go and have fun."

But all the confidence I'd shown with my mother drained away as Mike and I walked to the bus stop. I was very aware that he was shorter than me, not a lot shorter, but a few inches. The two of us going somewhere alone together made it *seem* like a date. And the whole idea of a date made me tongue-tied and brain-dead. The only date I'd ever been on had been to the junior high graduation dance in Iowa. I'd gone with a boy from my math class whose mother must have made him ask me. He didn't look up from his shoes all evening, except once when I spilled punch all over my dress. He kept apologizing, as though it was his fault, and pretty soon I started to believe it *was* his fault. I excused myself to clean up in the ladies' room, and sat in there for forty-five minutes so there was less time left to have to talk to him.

I imagine Mike felt a little awkward at first, too, but Mike was not a shoe-looker. "Red leaves on that maple," he announced, pointing. "Won't be long now. As you know, I'm not a great fan of New England, but this autumn-leaf-color business is all right."

A subject on which I had a definite opinion. "Oh, no, not you too! Everybody acts like New England is the only place in the world where leaves change color."

"You forget, I've only seen this once before. There's not much of a show in New Mexico, or California or Florida either."

"Well, let me assure you, the entire middle section of the country is full of trees that change color. New England does not have a monopoly on maple leaves."

"I bow to your superior knowledge. So, you hate it here, huh?"

I looked at him, surprised. "No, I don't hate it. I guess it doesn't affect me much. I could probably live anywhere."

He nodded. "Because you live inside your head. Me too. What kind of art do you do? Painting? Music?"

"What makes you think I do some kind of art?"

He shrugged. "You just seem like that kind of person."

"Well, I've never exactly thought of myself as an

artist. Of course, I read all the time. And I . . . write things." I couldn't believe I'd said that out loud. I never told people about writing. I didn't even tell my parents. It was a secret thing that I did just for myself. I hid the notebooks in the bottom of my desk drawer.

"A writer! Terrific! What do you write? Poetry, I bet."

"Why do you say that? Because I'm a girl? Girls write poetry?"

"Touchy, touchy. It so happens that I like poetry. I've tried to write it myself, but I'm no good."

"Well, I'm not much good either. But it's not the only thing I write. I've tried stories too, and plays. I think I'm best at the plays. I never show them to anyone, though, so don't even ask!"

"Why? You don't show them because you're not great or something? Jeez, you're just a kid. What do you expect?"

"I expect to be good before I show anybody!" It was funny. I wouldn't have said I took my writing all that seriously, but talking to Mike, I suddenly felt passionate about it.

"Someday I want to see it, okay? Let me know when it's ready."

"Don't hold your breath. Now tell me what you do, since obviously you're an artist too."

He smiled and shook his hair back. He had very soft-looking brown hair that kept falling down into his face. "I take pictures, photographs. For now. But eventually, I want to make movies. My dad has a video camera that he won't let me get my hands on. But I intend to talk him into it very soon."

"Really? You think you could make a movie?"

"Why not? Everybody has to do something — you ought to do the thing you love most. Hey, why don't you write a screenplay and I'll film it?"

All the way into the theater we talked about what kind of movie we'd make if we could. I totally forgot all that silly stuff about how to act with a boy and whether or not we were on a date. It just didn't matter, because talking to Mike was like talking to myself — easy and natural.

After the movies we were really psyched and not ready to go right home. Mike suggested we roam through a bookstore or two before heading back.

"The thing about Hitchcock is, the movies are actually based on a simple premise. The world is perfectly normal and then one odd thing happens, you see something strange, and then everything else begins to destruct around that one strange event." Mike couldn't stop talking. "Man, his cinematography is great too. The colors are weird; the people are beautiful but odd. Just everything. He's a master!"

"Well, I've always liked Hitchcock too, but have you ever seen any movies by François Truffaut? He's a French filmmaker and at the University . . ."

"I *love* Truffaut! *The 400 Blows, The Wild Child, Day For Night.*"

He had named my three favorite Truffaut movies. But rather than be amazed, I was a little miffed. Wasn't there anything I knew about that this kid didn't?

"You know," Mike continued. "Truffaut loved Hitchcock! You remember the scene in *Day for Night . . .*"

"With the books, I know. How about Godard? Have you ever seen *Alphaville?*"

"Godard? No, but I know about him. Tell me about it."

At last. The story of *Alphaville* took us through two bookstores, with frequent stops to examine screenplays we admired along the way. Just as we were leaving Bookmaster, I heard someone say, "Hello, Justine."

I never know anybody, so I could hardly believe it was for me, but I looked around anyway, and there was Jennifer Wolodny standing next to a very tall boy, or maybe I'd even have to call him a man.

"Hi, Jennifer. What are you doing here?"

"Oh, we often come into Cambridge on the weekends to look through the bookstores. This is my friend Peter Marquette. He goes to Harvard."

Peter smiled, a bit embarrassed, I thought. But then, not as embarrassed as I was.

"Oh, hi," I said. "This is my friend Mike Lombardo . . ."

Mike gave his biggest, silliest grin. "And I go to Allerton Junior High School!"

Part of me understood that this was very funny. It put down old Jennifer and her Harvard boyfriend and said who cares about all that? But part of me felt like a little kid bumming around with another little kid, acting silly. I couldn't decide which impulse to follow, so I guess I just stood there gawking.

"Well, we have to run," Jennifer said. "We're meeting some friends for dinner."

"Yeah," Mike nodded. "We gotta go too. My mom's probably waiting for me. It's almost my bedtime."

When Jennifer had hightailed it down the street, I turned on Mike. "Laying it on a little thick, weren't you?"

"Did I embarrass you? Is she your friend?"

"No, not really. She's one of the few people I speak to at school, though. I can't believe she goes out with that guy."

"I hate all that bragging about college stuff. That really galls me."

"She is kind of smart. Maybe she could go with a college guy."

"She may be smart, but she's a jerk. Acting like such a big shot. If you're in high school, act like it."

48

I couldn't help liking the kid. "Is there anything you don't have an opinion on?"

"I don't think so."

"If you're in junior high, act like it."

"That, of course, does not apply to me. I *am* older than I am." He pointed his chin and walked to the bus stop. Happily, I followed.

Chapter Ten

"So, were you baby-sitting for that kid, or what?" Jennifer Wolodny plunked her tray down next to mine.

"What kid?" I couldn't remember the last time I'd agreed to baby-sit.

"Saturday. In Harvard Square. That goofy kid."

Embarrassment fought with anger as I understood what she meant. "He's my neighbor. He likes to go to the movies," I said, hoping to get away without a full explanation.

"So you have to take him? I hope they pay you."

How could I tell her I couldn't even go myself unless he went with me? But when I looked into her smug, unfriendly face, it was clear to me where my loyalty had to be. "You don't get it. I go to the movies with him because I like to. He knows more about movies than anybody else I've met around here."

Jennifer stared at me, confused. "You mean he's, like, your friend?"

"Yeah. He's a neat kid, very smart." Admitting this to Jennifer made me feel suddenly in charge of the whole situation. I could say anything I wanted to, and if I just acted proud of it instead of ashamed of it, she'd have to accept it. "As a matter of fact, we've been talking about making a movie together."

"You're making a movie with a junior high kid?"

"I told you, he's not just some dumb kid."

"You doing this to combat your nerd image?"

"My what?"

"Nerd image. You know, everybody thinks you're kind of a social outcast brain." She spooned a gloppy pudding into her mouth.

I was speechless. I'd always thought of myself as sort of a romantic loner type, the female James Dean. Well, not quite so misunderstood. But never a nerd!

"Although I don't know why you'd bother," Jennifer continued. "Anyone who can't giggle twelve hours a day is a nerd in this Cesspool of Ignorance."

"So, does that make you a nerd too?" I asked.

She stuffed her trash into a brown bag. "I defy easy characterization," she bragged. "So tell me, is this kid your boyfriend or something?"

I knew I was blushing. Where did she get off with this stuff? "No, he's not my boyfriend, Jennifer. I wouldn't think someone who reads so much poetry would be so narrow-minded."

That got her. She sat up and started slurping down chocolate milk. "I was just asking," she mumbled.

I decided to get it over with. "So, was that *your* boyfriend, the guy from Harvard?" I'd change the subject and let her gloat a little.

But she didn't look so pleased. "Well, sort of. I mean, I've known him forever. We hang out together."

"How'd you meet him?"

She put her milk down. "Well, his parents and my parents are old friends. When he came to Harvard, my folks started inviting him out for dinner and things. So we got to be friends."

"So you're not exactly dating him."

"Not really."

"So was he baby-sitting for you on Saturday?" It was mean, I admit. But I just couldn't stop myself. Fortunately Jennifer's dormant sense of humor stirred itself a little. She definitely got the point.

"He takes me to the bookstores because I know so much about books." She gave me a half-smile then, and I thought maybe old Jennifer isn't so bad after all.

"By the way, I brought you some books to look at." She pulled two well-read volumes from her backpack and placed them before me. "Sylvia Plath and Elizabeth Bishop. If you have trouble with them, read them out loud. Plath is my favorite."

"Didn't she kill herself or something?"

"God, that's all anybody remembers about her!"

"Well, it's something you don't forget once you hear it."

Jennifer Wolodny pulled the books away from me, even though I'd opened the Plath book and was already looking through it.

"If you're only interested in an author because of the scandal surrounding her life, I suggest you turn on *Geraldo* rather than tax your brain!"

"I didn't say that!" I pulled the books back over to my side. "Gee, you'd think you were related to these people. They're a couple of dead writers." I may have been trying to provoke her here.

"How can you say that? These people had gifts that we can't even comprehend!"

"Well, I certainly can't comprehend them if you don't let me look at the books!"

I suppose we were getting a bit rowdy. Suddenly Jennifer Holtz stood up noisily, scraping her chair across the floor. She stuck her book under her arm, grabbed her tray full of dishes, and stomped off to another table, muttering under her breath.

"I don't think we were being very respectful of Stephen King," I said, bowing my head.

Jennifer Wolodny, my new friend, laughed.

Chapter Eleven

"It makes no sense." Dad shook his head sadly as the lights went up in the theater. "Walt Disney's *Beauty and the Beast* gets an Academy Award nomination and *this* is overlooked."

Dad had found a movie theater in Somerville that specialized in cult films, and he'd talked me into going to see *Edward Scissorhands* again. It was one of his recent favorites, and he'd seen it half a dozen times, most of them with me. He says it's a classic, full of pathos and symbolism, but at the same time screamingly hilarious. I admit, the scene with the waterbed breaks me up every time.

"It's too sophisticated for the Academy Awards, Dad. Actually, this is a very weird movie." I tried to cheer him up.

"Nominations shouldn't go to the movies that make the most money, or have the biggest budgets, or . . ." He was off and running. He sounded angry, but actually I knew he loved pontificating like this, and I was his favorite audience. I was half listening as we moved outside through the crowd.

"Hi, Justine!" I felt a tap on my shoulder and turned to find Heather Lombardo and Jackson Demuth wrapped around each other.

"Hi. What are you doing here?"

"Are you kidding? I love Johnny Depp! Don't you think Jackson looks kind of like him?" She smiled up into the big guy's face and he flipped his hair back as though he couldn't be bothered being compared to teenage idols.

"Maybe," I hedged as my stomach flopped around. I hated the excited feeling I got around this gift-to-women jerk.

"Well, hello. Aren't you the girl across the street?" Dad extended a hand to Heather and she looked at it as though he held out an octopus.

"This is my dad. Heather. Jackson." I made the intros as brief as possible. What fifteen-year-old girl goes to the movies on a Saturday night with her father? I mean, actually, I do, quite a bit, but we usually go to movies where I wouldn't expect to meet anyone I know. I figured this news would put me over the top in the Nerd Olympics.

The Couple giggled off down the street and Dad and I walked around the corner to the car.

"You want to get an ice cream before we go home?" Dad asked.

"I don't think so. I'm not in the mood."

"Did it embarrass you to be with your father when we saw those kids?" That's Dad. Cut to the chase.

"Not exactly. I'm not embarrassed by you or anything. It's just that kids think it's kind of geeky to go places with your parents."

"You'd rather be with a boy?"

"No. I mean, what boy would I be with? I don't know anybody who'd ask me that I'd want to go with."

"You go to the movies with Heather's brother sometimes."

"That's different. He's a kid."

Dad couldn't stifle a small laugh. "Two years younger, isn't he? Someday two years won't seem like anything."

"Well, they seem like a lot now. I mean, he's kind of fun for a kid, but he's not even in high school yet. And anyway, it's not like a date when I go with him. It's just friends."

"That's what it should be at your age anyway. Just friends."

I sighed. "I know. That's what Mom says too. Unfortunately nobody seems to have told the rest of the teenage world."

"Mom gets worried about you not having many friends."

"Are you worried?"

Dad smiled at me. "No, I'm not. The thing is,

you're not run-of-the-mill. You're a little different. So were Mom and I at your age; she's forgotten how it is. If you're not the pep-rally type, you don't see immediately where you fit in. But there are plenty of other kinds of people in the world. You'll make your friends and they'll be *real* friends."

"I'm not really worried, either. Actually, I do have one other friend besides Mike. A girl I eat lunch with. She reads poetry. She's kind of obnoxious, but she's interesting."

"Sounds like just your type."

We walked along silently for a minute and then suddenly Dad burst out. "Wasn't Diane Wiest great? An Avon lady meeting her greatest challenge. How did they come up with that idea? It's brilliant! God, I wish I could write like that. I still want to make a movie someday!"

He wasn't really talking to me anymore. He was dreaming again. I was glad he dreamed out loud so I could listen. I decided I'd let him take me for ice cream after all.

Chapter Twelve

"That is the dumbest movie, Mike. Isn't there something else we could see tomorrow?"

"Dumb? Are you kidding? This was the granddaddy of all space movies! There wouldn't have been any *Star Wars* without it!"

"What a loss." It was Friday afternoon and Mike and I were walking home from school together, a habit we'd gotten into lately, trying to decide what to see the next day. I wasn't crazy about any space movies, but *2001: A Space Odyssey* was the worst of the lot, as far as I was concerned. "You ought to go with my dad. He loves it; that's why I've been forced to see it three times already."

"The set, the pacing, the music . . ."

"The boredom! Really, let's pick something else." It wasn't easy to find a Saturday movie unless the Brattle was running classics. So many of the new movies were either rated R or made for nincompoops.

Mike scanned the movie ads as we walked. "There isn't anything else in Cambridge."

I scowled. "It's humorless, that's the problem. I mean, it ought to be kind of funny, with that goofy-looking computer with the sweet voice, but it never is. It's just endless. Somebody ought to do a spoof of it."

No sooner had the words left my mouth than ideas began to flash through my mind. It could be hilarious! A girl and her idiotic computer. They're best friends. They discuss everything. They comb each other's hair. The computer could be a big doll. The girl gets jealous of the computer. The possibilities were endless. I stopped in my tracks and Mike walked on a few steps, then stopped and looked back at me.

"What's the matter?"

"I've got it. *2001: A Space Oddball.* It'll be very funny. I'll write it and you film it!"

For a minute he said nothing. Then, "Okay. maybe. Who's in it?"

"A girl and a computer. That's all."

"A-huh. Computer's name should be a takeoff on HAL."

"It's a girl computer, so . . . HALICE!"

"Which stands for . . . highly adequate, highly accurate . . ."

"Highly accurate little . . ."

"The *C* could stand for computer."

"Highly accurate little something computer something. I don't know. It should be funny. I'll look through the dictionary."

"Okay. So what happens?"

"I'm not sure yet. They're best friends, but the real girl gets jealous of the computer."

"Why?"

"Because the computer gets better grades?"

"No, that's to be expected. Something funnier."

"Right. Because the computer has better hair? Has a cuter boyfriend?"

"Something like that, yeah. Even though the computer is 'smart,' being a computer and all, it's still ditzy, like the girl!"

"That's just what I thought! The thing is, you can order a computer that's just like you!"

"Model the ditzy girl on my sister. You can't go wrong."

"Mike!"

"Write it! Write it tonight and let me see it tomorrow!"

"I don't think I can write the whole thing that fast!"

"Well, as much as you can. My dad is supposed to be home tonight. I'll work on him to let me use the video camera. I think he's coming around, especially if I make it sound like this is a project I'm working on with an older kid, like it's not just some childish thing."

I laughed. "You may be young, but I never think of you as childish. I'd almost say you're a very old person inside a young body."

Mike gave me a long look, which was kind of embarrassing. I had to look away. "That's how I feel a lot of the time too. But my dad wouldn't know it. Even when he's around he's too busy to figure out who I am."

We didn't talk too much the rest of the way home. I was thinking about ideas for the script. I couldn't be sure if Mike was thinking about the movie or his father, but when we parted in front of our houses, he said, "Get to work!"

And I did. As a matter of fact, I couldn't stop myself. It was crazy, the ideas came so fast. Since I didn't have anybody there to help me decide which ideas were good and which were stupid, I'd put them to the "Mike" test, trying to imagine what his reaction would be.

Mom had to call me three times for supper and finally came up to get me.

"What are you so engrossed in that you aren't hungry for beef stew with gravy?"

"I'm writing this screenplay." I expected that to raise her eyebrows, and it did.

"Screenplay? What brought this on?"

"Mike wants to make a movie, and he asked me to write him a screenplay. So I got an idea this afternoon, and I want to get it down."

"That's great, hon. Can I see it?"

"Not yet. I want to get it all done before I show anybody."

She was disappointed. I think it's hard for mothers when their kids stop running to them to show off every little word and picture they come up with. For years they have to pretend to be interested in everything you do, and then just when the stuff gets kind of interesting, you don't really want to show it all to them.

"Well, come down to dinner now," she said sternly. "You don't have to finish this immediately."

As I was rushing through dinner, the phone rang. It was Mike. "2021. We should move it up a little because 2001 is too close. It should still be in the future."

"You're right. 2021, you think, or farther ahead?"

"I like 2021. It keeps the same sounds in it."

"Okay. See you tomorrow."

"Are you working on it now?"

"I just paused for dinner. My mother insisted."

"But get right back to it after!"

My mother was a little shocked that I refused a dish of mint chocolate chip ice cream to go back upstairs and work. The thing was, I knew Mike was counting on me to write this now, and I felt I couldn't be another person who'd let him down.

Chapter Thirteen

"This is great! This is great! You're a great writer!" Mike kept hitting the pages while I grinned foolishly. It was the first time my writing had faced an audience, and Mike's reaction couldn't have been better. "I love HALICE!" he kept shouting.

We'd gone in to see the early matinee of *2001*, just to jog our memories, in case there was anything to make fun of that we'd forgotten, and then came back to Mike's house to work. It was his idea to use the balcony off Heather's room.

I'd told him, of course, how I'd fallen in love with the place and thought of that balcony as mine, so it had become our unofficial meeting place. As Mike said, Heather's never home, anyway, and the only thing she ever used the balcony for was drying her nylons. My mom still wasn't crazy about my spending so much time with Mike, but if I said we were on the balcony, it must have seemed safer, like we were outside or something. And Mike's mother never bothered her kids at all. As a matter of fact, she hardly spoke to them, just sat in the TV room and read magazines, or that's all I ever saw her do.

I admit I felt kind of funny about traipsing through Heather's room all the time, especially because I couldn't help gawking at all her stuff. She had so many clothes she couldn't get the closet door shut, and there were about forty shoes to step over — none of which seemed to match — in order to get to the balcony. She had one of those dressers with a little stool in front of it, the kind you think of old-movie stars sitting in front of while they pile on the makeup. I guess Heather had seen the same movies, because the top of the dresser was stacked with red tubes and bottles of goo. It looked like an army of starlets lived in that place.

"Highly Advertised, Lovely, Insipid Computer with Emotions. It's great. Will everybody know what insipid means? Should you say idiotic?"

"You know what it means, don't you?"

"Of course I do!" Mike looked insulted.

"Well, the movie's not for little kids. People our age will get it."

Our age. As I said it the words kind of hung in the air, and they stayed there after I finished talking. Was there an "our age"? On the one hand Mike really didn't seem younger than me; he was at least as smart, maybe smarter. And he didn't act silly like so many boys his age, or even older guys.

64

But still he was shorter than me and thin, and sometimes I'd imagine what we looked like walking along together, a tall girl and this short kid. He probably looked like my younger brother. Well, that was O.K. I certainly didn't want anyone thinking he was my boyfriend. Even though — and this I could hardly admit even to myself — I'd started to think he was kind of good-looking. He had a nice smile and, as I've said before, great hair. And these eyes. He had this habit of looking right at me, right in my eyes, that could make me blush, unless I looked away immediately and started talking.

"You know what I want to do? Let's work on the computer, make it. We've got lots of extra boxes left over from the move. The way I see HALICE, there are long gloves, like . . . kitchen mitts that stick out from her sides, so somebody can be behind her with their arms through the gloves to make her actually able to do things."

"But I thought of HALICE as a kind of doll," I interrupted.

"Doll." He thought it over, shaking his head. "Not the body. We wouldn't be able to move it. But maybe the head. Yes! Down in the basement there's this big old doll that was Heather's. I don't know how it survived the move, but I saw it leaning in a corner down there. We'll use her head."

"Won't Heather mind?"

65

"Heather has no mind. Besides, she's well past the age of playing with dolls."

We spent the next hour or so working on HALICE, taping boxes together and scavenging various body parts. Suddenly I realized that the sun was disappearing.

"Oh! I promised my mom I'd be home by dark so I could help her with tonight's dinner. Your family's coming over."

"I know. I hope your parents aren't expecting much. I mean, my folks are downright weird."

"Weird?"

"You'll see."

*   *   *

They didn't seem weird when they came in the door, just a little distracted. Mom bustled around and took their coats. Mr. Lombardo thanked Mom and then complimented her on her dress, even though he was looking around the living room while he said it.

Mrs. Lombardo kept looking down at her own outfit, which was very pretty but a little too dressy, I thought, to wear across the street to dinner with the neighbors. It was a black woolen suit with a white silk blouse underneath that had big ruffles all around the collar and down the front. Like she was going to a fancy restaurant. And she had on those three-inch heels that Mom doesn't even own and I can't imagine how people walk in.

Heather and Mike were sort of quiet, though Heather gave me a big smile and Mike saluted. It was hard to know what to say to them in front of all our parents. Thank goodness Mike had on the same jeans and shirt he'd worn that afternoon — at least he didn't look like a stranger. And Heather was wearing one of her usual gorgeous getups, which always made me feel that my perfectly normal clothes were terribly ugly.

We sat around the living room eating stuffed mushrooms and baba ganoosh for about half an hour. Dad got Mr. Lombardo to tell him a little about his work, although I couldn't really get the gist of it. He was mostly interested in talking about all the great places he got to travel on business. Dad had been to a couple of the same places, so they had that to talk about.

Mom was trying real hard with Mrs. Lombardo. She kept saying, "Justine tells me you moved here from Connecticut," and "Justine says the moving around has been difficult for you," until I felt like a spy. Mrs. L. was very polite, but she answered Mom's questions in as few syllables as possible every time.

"I'd be happy to introduce you to a few people in town," Mom offered. "Not that I'm really into the social scene here, but working at the library, I do meet people. You might want to have lunch with me someday; there's a nice coffee shop just down the block from the library."

Mrs. Lombardo smiled and seemed to really look at Mom for the first time. "Well, thank you. That might be fun. I've . . . hardly gotten around town at all, to see what's here . . ."

A booming laugh came from Mr. Lombardo. "What! Don't tell me you're actually going to leave the house and *do* something? Mrs. Trainor doesn't realize she's witnessing a miracle here!"

A curtain closed over Mrs. L.'s face and she looked down into her lap. For a minute I thought she might cry, but then she rearranged her face and smiled. "Perhaps you could join me for lunch at my home someday. It's a little difficult for me to get out."

Mr. L. continued to snort and snicker. I could tell Mom didn't know what to say. It would be kind of crazy to drive all the way back here to have lunch across the street from her own house and then drive back to work for the afternoon. But finally she said, yes, maybe she could do that sometime. After that, nobody knew where to look, so Mom hurried us into the dining room sooner than she would have otherwise.

Once the chicken cordon bleu and the rice pilaf had made the rounds, and everybody had exclaimed politely over their first bite, an uncomfortable silence surrounded the table. I should have known that a parent in distress is likely to turn on her child, but I didn't see it coming.

"Well," Mom said brightly, "isn't it nice that Justine and Mike have become such good friends? They're practically *inseparable*."

That would have been enough right there, with the implication that there was some kind of romance going on, but then the Lombardos went Mom one better.

"Oh, I think it's so sweet that your daughter has befriended little Mike. He's had such a hard time making friends with the boys," Mrs. L. said timidly. I glanced across the table at Mike as his eyes widened and grew angry.

"Hell, Margaret!" Mr. L. shouted. "Give the boy some credit. He knows a good-looking chick when he sees one! I always liked older women myself." Mr. Lombardo winked at me.

When Heather laughed, she actually sprayed milk across her plate.

Mike scraped his chair back from the table and stood up. "I am not 'little Mike,' and please don't give me any credit, Dad. Please." He stalked to the front door and banged out.

I was impressed. I wanted out of there too, but without Mike's example I probably wouldn't have had the nerve. I stood up, although with less anger.

"I've lost my appetite too. Good night, everybody." Mom looked up in surprise, wondering, I'm sure, how her lovely dinner party had gotten so strange. Mike's weird family. He was right. As I reached my bedroom, I heard the doorbell ring. It was Jackson Demuth coming to pick up Heather. At my house. Jackson Demuth was standing in my house, talking to my mother, but not the least bit interested in me. I slammed the bedroom door as hard as I could.

Chapter Fourteen

I stayed inside all day Sunday. I didn't call Mike
and he didn't call me. On Monday morning, as she
drove me to school, Mom was still apologizing and
explaining and trying to figure out what happened.

"I didn't mean to embarrass you . . . I guess I
wasn't thinking how it would sound to you, but,
honey, you know, you *know* . . ."

"I know, Mom. You can stop telling me."

"Oh, and I feel so sorry for Margaret. She's such
a shy person, and that husband of hers making fun
of her like that. No wonder she can't get over her
problems. She has no support."

I could tell Mom was deciding to make it her
business to be Mrs. L.'s one-woman support group.
I wasn't sure how this might affect me or Mike, but
I decided he probably would never speak to me
again, anyway, so what difference did it make?

"You know, I'll bet she's agoraphobic. I'm sure
that must be it. Didn't you say she doesn't go anywhere?"

"That's what Mike says."

"Maybe she could go out with me. If I drove. I'm going to ask her to go shopping with me next weekend."

Mom dropped me off and drove away, still plotting her good works. It was a warm morning and kids were standing around in groups waiting for the bell to ring. Kids from my classes usually said hi, but I never felt I could just go up and join in their groups. Then I heard someone call, "Over here! Justine!"

Jennifer Wolodny sat on the top step of the library building and patted the concrete beside her. It was such a normal thing to do, but it made me exceedingly happy that somebody was saving this hard seat for me.

"Hi," I said, sitting down. "What are you up to?"

"Waiting for the building to open, so I can return some books. Speaking of which . . ."

"I know, I've got your books. And I've read some in each of them. The Bishop is a little harder, but the Plath book I really like. I mean, I don't exactly understand whole poems, but she *sounds* so great. I like to read them out loud."

"Do you? So do I. Maybe some afternoon we could get together and read poetry!"

"Sure. Except I'm sort of in the middle of this project right now, with somebody."

"What is it?"

"Well, we're making a movie. A video. You'd

72

probably think it was dumb. It's a takeoff on *2001: A Space Odyssey.*"

"You're making a movie? With whom, might I ask?" She did have an obnoxious way of talking.

I sighed. "A friend."

"No! You're making a movie with that junior high kid, aren't you? I don't get it. What's so great about this kid?"

"Nothing!" I said, anger building. Why did everybody act like Mike and I were such a cute and funny little team, they couldn't bear not to make fun of us? Because I was so nerdy? Because I couldn't get a real boyfriend? Who wanted one anyway?

Jennifer shrugged. "Hey, I'm not knocking it. God knows there aren't any intelligent male life forms on this campus."

I calmed myself down. "You'd probably like Mike too, if you knew him." Suddenly inspiration struck. "Maybe you could help us! We're going to need a girl to move the robot around and to be the voice for it. I'm the ditzy real girl, so I can't be both. And your voice would be perfect: sort of nasal and a little snotty."

"Oh, thank you so much. How can I turn down such an offer? My debut as a snotty robot. Hollywood calls. There's a huge salary, I presume?"

"It'll be fun. I'll talk to Mike after school and see what he thinks." If he's speaking to me, I thought.

"Oh, yes, don't offer me the job until I audition

for the almighty Mike." She sounded annoyed, but I was learning how to read Jennifer. She was pleased, possibly even thrilled that I'd asked her. She wasn't exactly beating off friends with a stick either.

I was more than a little happy to see Mike waiting for me in the usual spot as I came out of school. He acted like he didn't see me coming so he wouldn't have to smile. I walked right up to him and he acted surprised to see me. The Great Pretender, but I let it go.

"Hey," he said. "Ready to work on HALICE?"

"Sure." Obviously the less said about Saturday night the better.

As we walked home I told him my idea about using Jennifer as the voice and movement for HALICE.

He looked dubious. "Couldn't we just do it ourselves? Do we have to get somebody else involved? I don't even know her."

"We need another person. We can't use my voice for the girl and the robot. It'll be too confusing. She's okay. Besides, you did meet her. She was the girl we ran into in Harvard Square with that Harvard guy."

"Her? Jeez, what a snot! I thought you didn't like her. I thought you didn't have any friends."

"I don't, just you and this one other snot. Look, she's just defensive, a free-thinker type. Like us. She's okay.

"Right. She didn't make fun of the fact that you're making a movie with a junior high kid?"

"She did at first. But she came around."

He sighed. "I'll meet her, but I'm not making any promises."

"Thank you, Mr. Zanuck."

*   *   *

We were out on Heather's balcony, sewing the kitchen mitts to the sleeves of an old shirt, which we would then glue onto the robot-box-body, when Heather came flying into her room. I must say, she never seemed to mind that Mike and I had taken over her balcony.

"Hi you two," she called. "Justine, I'm glad you're here! I wanted to talk to you."

This was a switch. These days I seemed to be primarily invisible to Heather. Not that she was a snob exactly, just too busy with her big circle of friends to pay any attention to anybody else.

"How'd you like to double-date with us next Friday night?"

I opened my mouth to reply, but no sound came out. It wasn't a question I knew how to respond to, but Heather continued.

"Alex Lieberman asked Jackson to get him a date, and Jackson thought you might like to come. Do you know Alex? He's a little shy, I guess."

Shy wasn't the first word that came to mind when I thought of Alex Lieberman. He was one of Jack-

75

son's friends, though not as good-looking, and he'd always seemed like one of those sausage-fingered guys who lunge for girls as though they're footballs. He wasn't all that popular, but he could certainly pass, since he was one of Jackson's friends. Anyway, how could I turn down a chance to double-date with Jackson and Heather? It wasn't done, and certainly not by somebody who'd never had a real date in her life.

"Yeah, I know him. He's in my geometry class."

"Well, he's probably not as smart as you, and all, but he was real excited when Jackson suggested you. How about it?"

"Well, sure, I guess so." He was excited? Jackson suggested me?

"Great. Jackson will pick Alex up first and then come and get us about seven. We'll go to a movie and then out somewhere, okay?"

"Yeah. Thanks for asking me." I sounded wimpy, even to me, and I could imagine Mike looking disgusted.

Heather breezed out. "Anytime!"

When I turned around though, it was more like anger than disgust I saw on Mike's face.

"I can't believe I just heard that."

"What?"

"You're double-dating with my idiot sister and her bozo boyfriend and some gorilla he picked out for you?"

76

"He's not a gorilla."

"Oh, he's a real prince, I bet. A football star?"

"I guess he does play football."

"Oh, well, you have arrived. Just to be seen in this sterling company! Next thing I know you'll be trying out for cheerleader."

"You're being ridiculous," I said, but I had to admit part of the reason I wanted to go was to be seen with this group. I really had no interest in Alex Lieberman at all. "You're too hard on Heather. And Jackson too."

Mike's jaw dropped down to the middle of his chest and his eyes popped wildly. "I can't believe you're saying this! You like that Jackson guy?"

I couldn't exactly admit to that. "I know he's not a mental giant, but he can be very nice . . ."

"And he looks like a stud." Mike got right to the point.

"You hate him because he's gorgeous?"

"Gorgeous? You think he's gorgeous?"

"He's good-looking, all right?"

"So, would you go out with some guy just because he's good-looking, even if he had nothing else going for him?"

"Maybe."

"I can't believe this!"

"Maybe once. I didn't say I'd marry him!"

"Would you *not* go out with somebody because he was bad-looking?"

I hesitated. "How bad?"

"You're a jerk! I can't believe this. How come I didn't know before this you were a jerk?"

"I am not. You're asking me dumb questions. Are we talking about if I had my choice of every guy in the world?"

Mike glared at me. "So, I guess now you and Heather are going to be bosom buddies?"

"What's the matter with you? It's one night. Can't I be the slightest bit normal? I have to be a nerdy nut like you or else you won't have anything to do with me?"

As soon as the words were out, I regretted them. I could tell by the way Mike's face twitched that my words had hurt him. I felt so confused. The last thing I wanted was to hurt Mike, but couldn't he give me some leeway here? This was a chance I couldn't refuse and he couldn't understand. So I turned around and ran. Ran home and buried myself in Sylvia Plath poems.

Chapter Fifteen

I didn't so much as catch a glimpse of Mike all that week. Not that I expected to. It was a very long week, and the closer it got to Friday, the more I regretted saying I would go on this date.

Every time I passed Heather at school, she'd wink at me, like we had some great secret or something. Or like she was my sorority sister doing me a big favor. Once I saw Jackson, and he gave me a thumbs-up signal from across the hall. What had I gotten myself into, hanging around with these glamorous phonies?

When I told Jennifer about my date, she was almost as bad as Mike.

"Alex Lieberman? You're not serious? That pea-brain? Why do you want to go out with him?"

"I don't! I just thought I ought to go out with *somebody,* and this is the first offer that's come along."

She shook her head. "From what I hear, you better wear a heavy coat and keep it buttoned up tight."

"What do you mean?"

She gave me a look.

"He's fast?" I asked.

"Faster than a speeding bullet, according to the grapevine."

"But Heather said he liked me." Didn't she say that? Or not? "Maybe he won't try anything on the first date."

"Yeah. Maybe the leaves won't fall off the trees this fall."

By Friday night I was so nervous I couldn't eat any dinner.

"You ought to have something, sweetie," Mom cajoled. "How about a peanut butter sandwich? That won't upset your stomach."

"My stomach is not upset. I'm just not hungry." I sat on the living room couch, staring at the front door, willing the thing to begin so I could see how bad it would be and get it over with.

"Don't worry about her, Jean. Didn't you get nervous the first time you went out with somebody? I think I cut my face to pieces shaving the first time I took you out."

Oh, I hated hearing these cute stories about their early lives together. It always sounded so perfect, more perfect than my life could ever be.

A horn honked and I raced to the door, grabbing my coat.

"I guess it's too much to expect a modern boy to actually come to the door and meet your parents." Dad sighed, rising from his chair.

"You're not coming out to the car with me, are you?" I asked, alarmed.

"Relax. It'll give you something to talk about. How old-fashioned your father is." Dad took his jacket off the hook by the door and I could see it was pointless to argue. He walked me to the car.

Heather had already jumped into the front seat with Jackson, and the back door was standing open, waiting for me. Inside sat Alex Lieberman, who had obviously not cut himself shaving in preparation for this date. He probably hadn't even looked in a mirror; his hair was uncombed and stuck up oddly on one side.

"Hello, kids," Dad greeted them. The two in the front seat said hello back, but Alex Lieberman just ducked his head, like he couldn't see or imagine who could be speaking.

"Don't worry, Mr. Trainor," Jackson said. "We'll be back by midnight. That okay?"

"Well, that's all right, I guess. You must be Alex," Dad said, practically crawling into the back seat.

"Yup," my date replied. Shy.

"Nice to meet you," said my old-fashioned dad.

"Yup."

Dad straightened up. "Drive carefully, will you kids?"

"Oh, sure, Mr. Trainor," Jackson said. Heather

winked. That wink seemed to be her major form of communication.

Jackson drove off sedately, turned the corner, and roared away. I was thrown back against the seat, against Alex Lieberman.

I swear he snickered, but I couldn't even look at him. I just kept thinking, What am I doing in this car and how soon can I get back home?

It seemed the group had decided on a movie without me and we were going to see Arnold Schwarzenegger, whether I liked it or not. I hate Arnold Schwarzenegger movies. But once we were settled in our theater seats, I felt myself calming down a little. After all, what could happen? We'd see the movie, probably go for something to eat, and go home. No big deal. I'd never have to go out with this speechless moron again. Of course, it would make Heather and Jackson mad, and I didn't really want to be their enemy. After all, Jackson had been nice to arrange this date with his friend, even if I didn't happen to like him.

I decided to make the best of it. Maybe Alex really was shy and underneath that stupid exterior lay a human being.

"Want some popcorn?" he bleated in my ear.

Well, that was considerate of him, wasn't it? "Sure, thanks."

Alex and Jackson went out for refreshments. It seemed like I ought to talk to Heather, but I couldn't think of a thing to say, and when I looked her way, sure enough, she winked.

Arnold started pumping and sweating. Yuck. I ate popcorn. Suddenly Alex's arm plunged behind my shoulders and yanked me crooked in my seat. It was not comfortable. And somehow, watching Arnold sweating up there on the screen made me think that Alex's hand was sweating all over my blouse too. By the time the movie was finally over, I had a pain in my back from sitting at that crazy angle.

So, I thought, only a pizza or something to get through and then home.

But as soon as we were in the car, Alex found his voice. "Let's go to the lake, huh?"

The lake? Even a total social outcast like me knew what the lake meant. Parking, kissing, and as much sex as time, space, and your conscience will allow.

"Is that okay with you, Justine?" Heather murmured sweetly, as though I had any say in the matter. Jackson had already started the car and turned away from town. My fate was sealed.

"I guess so."

With those magic words, Alex grabbed me around the waist and pulled me close. His breath smelled like old hamburgers.

It didn't take long to get to the lake, not the way Jackson drove. He killed the lights and immediately jumped on Heather and started moaning and

83

groaning. Maybe this will be a learning experience, I said to myself. I'm not used to this kind of thing, but it's time I learned. I tried to gear myself up for it.

But then this greasy guy, who hadn't said six words to me all evening, leaned over and started kissing me, biting me even, biting my lips. "No, don't do that!" I said and pushed him back.

So he grabbed me farther down then, my breasts. He got my coat unbuttoned so fast I thought he must have popped the buttons. While he pulled at my bra, he started to suck on my neck. Jeez, it really hurt.

"Stop it! I don't want to do this!" I yelled, pushing him away again. Jackson and Heather turned around to see what was the matter. "Couldn't we just go somewhere and . . . talk or something?" I asked meekly.

"Oh, God," Jackson said and banged the steering wheel.

Alex was sort of puffing by then and really mad. "Jackson, I thought you said this girl was a piece of cake!"

I couldn't believe what I was hearing. "What?"

Jackson turned to me. "Well, that's the message I always got from you, Justine. That flirty little voice and blushing and pretending to be so shy!"

"I wasn't pretending! You got the wrong message!"

84

"I thought you said you liked Alex?" Heather said innocently.

"I didn't say that. I hardly know him. Would you take me home please?"

"Oh, jeez, now she wants to go home," Alex complained. "Thank you, Jackson, thanks a lot. You really can pick 'em."

"Listen, you crank," Jackson shot back. "You're lucky I could find anybody who'd go out with you at all. You're not number one on the hit parade, you know." Jackson put the car in gear and raced backward out of the parking space.

So what was I, thirty-fifth on the list of girls asked on this date? I was just feeling better and better all the time. What a fool I was!

Jackson was driving like a maniac, shouting insults back and forth with Alex. None of us was wearing a seat belt. Even though normally I always do, it had seemed too nerdy with this group. But now that they hated me anyway, I searched for the belt. A slight rain had begun to fall, and the way Jackson was driving I couldn't imagine making it home in one piece.

But before I could dig the thing out from under the seat, Jackson made good on my prediction, running a red light while he was turning around to scream at his pal, and we smashed into the side of another car, then spun around three times, before we stopped with two wheels up on the curb and a mailbox blocking Heather's door.

It seemed to take a long time, from the moment I could see we were going to hit that car until we finally stopped moving. I had been flung all over the back seat and hit my cheekbone on the door handle, but in the moment of silence after we stopped, I decided all my basic parts were still operational. I was so glad to be alive, and so anxious to get out of that car.

"Oh, I'm hurt," Heather moaned. "Help me!" Her head was lying on the back of the seat as though she couldn't move it.

The people in the other car must have been pretty bounced around too, but they got out before we did and the man started screaming.

"What the hell's the matter with you kids? Are you drunk? Are you on drugs? You could have killed us!"

"Calm down, Harvey," his wife said. "They might be hurt."

I opened my door and stumbled out, grabbing onto the woman a little bit. "I'm sorry," I said. "We're not drunk." Then I stumbled over to the side of the road and threw up, no doubt rendering my story unbelievable. By that time I could hear the police cars and the ambulance coming. I put my head down on my arms and waited. I could hear Jackson cursing and even arguing with Alex some more, so I figured we were at least all alive.

But when the ambulance arrived, Jackson yelled,

"In here! I think she's hurt and I'm afraid to try to move her!"

I stood up then and peered in the window. Heather was crying and there was blood running down her face from a big gash across her forehead. Because of the mailbox, the door on her side was wedged closed.

Even Alex looked scared. He didn't speak, but he paced up and down the sidewalk. He looked over at me once and said, "You okay? Your cheek's bloody."

"I'm fine," I said. "You?"

"Great, just great," he growled.

The ambulance workers were telling Jackson that in order to get Heather out of the car with the least trauma, they were going to have to break the gearshift lever on the floor.

"But how am I gonna drive the car?" Jackson asked, confused.

"Buddy, you ain't gonna drive this car, ever again. Take a good look at it."

He was right. The car was totaled. Jackson looked like he was going to cry, but then they started moving Heather out of the front seat, and he looked scared again. We all did.

Chapter Sixteen

Jackson and I rode in the ambulance with Heather. I lay down on the other stretcher, even though I didn't really need to, and Jackson sat in a seat next to Heather. He was pretty nice to her, though I doubt if she even knew it. She kept crying and moaning and wasn't too with it. I don't even know what happened to Alex. He wasn't hurt, so maybe he just went on home. I didn't care.

The lights in the emergency room were so bright they hurt my eyes. I had to lie down, staring straight up into the fluorescents while they checked me over and put four stitches in my cheek. I wasn't really thinking about anything, certainly not about old Alex, or about the accident, or even Heather. I was just kind of numb.

Even when Mom and Dad came running in with the Lombardos I didn't get too excited. We had to sign some forms, and the police kept walking around shaking their heads and saying, "You kids sure were lucky," which struck me as funny under the circumstances. But I guess they were right.

Mom and Dad looked very serious, but once they knew I was O.K. they started asking questions. Hadn't we been wearing seat belts? How fast had Jackson been driving? And why were we way out by the lake?

I just couldn't answer them. I put my hand up to my bandaged cheek and just said, "Don't worry, I'm okay." After a minute they relaxed and hugged me. Mom blinked back a few tears.

I could hear Mrs. Lombardo, though. She was wailing and hollering about "her baby" being hurt. Little by little I felt I was coming back to life. I wondered what was happening to the others.

"It seems that Jackson has a broken arm," Mom told me. "He didn't even realize it until he got here. And poor Heather seems to have both whiplash and a concussion. She's in quite a bit of pain right now, but they'll give her something for it. She'll have to stay in the hospital for at least a few days."

"Her mom doesn't sound too good."

"Margaret is very upset. If you're feeling all right, honey, maybe I should go and see if I can do something for her," Mom said.

"Sure. I'm okay."

"I need to fill out some insurance papers at the

desk," Dad said, giving me a kiss on the forehead. "I won't be long. Then we can get you home."

I sat alone on one of those high carts in my bright white cubicle, trying not to think, but now I was remembering the accident, that helpless feeling when you know it's going to happen. And you think, this is the last thing I'll ever do in my life.

I looked up when Mike appeared in the doorway. "Can I come in?" he asked quietly.

"Sure."

He walked a little closer. "Are you okay?"

"I think so."

"My parents were scared to death when the police called. I'm . . . glad you're okay."

"Yeah."

"You know, I'm sorry I acted so dumb about this whole thing."

"Are you kidding? You were right. Alex Lieberman sucks."

"I can see that." Mike smiled and pointed to the blue bruise on my neck.

I had to smile. "Very funny."

"Really, I'm glad you're okay."

"Can't you think of anything original to say?"

"When you've been a jerk, act like a jerk. Lombardo's Law." He smiled at me.

I meant to laugh at that, but for some reason I started to cry. I mean, the tears just poured down my face even though I wasn't making any noise.

Mike jumped up on the cart next to me. He took my hand in both of his and rubbed it very gently, the way you do with a little kid who's gotten slightly frostbitten. It was very nice, but I just kept on crying. I think I was crying about how lucky I was.

Chapter Seventeen

"Jean, I hope you know I really appreciate you coming with me on these trips." Mrs. Lombardo waited while Mom put her coat on.

"Don't be silly, Margaret! I've told you how glad I am to have a friend to do things with again. Once you get married and have children, you get so involved with your family, you forget how wonderful it is to get together with a woman friend and just *talk*."

Mike and I sat together at the dining room table, working on the screenplay. We rolled our eyes at each other. It seemed that for the last six weeks, since the accident, talking to each other was *all* our mothers did anymore.

"Dr. Blanchard says I'm making remarkable progress," Mrs. Lombardo reported. "Of course, I'm not ready to drive to Burlington by myself, but just the fact that I can get to the mall and walk around and shop without breaking into a cold sweat is a minor miracle. I'll tell you, sometimes I thought I'd never leave my house again."

Mom reached over and gave her a little hug. "I'm proud of you. And I'm glad you like Dr. Blanchard so well."

"Oh, yes. We talk about *everything*. He's been a tremendous help in dealing with Heather over this whole accident thing. And, to tell the truth, I even see some changes in Will. He's agreed to come with me next week."

"Either she doesn't think she needs help with me, or I'm already beyond hope," Mike whispered.

"You know, it's odd," Mom said as the two of them walked out the door, "but sometimes you remind me of my old friend Susan Marshall."

I had to laugh.

"What's so funny?"

"Poor Mom. She's been waiting twenty-five years to have a best friend move in across the street again."

"Yeah. It's nice, how they like each other. My mom is getting different. Better. She's not nearly so crazy anymore. Of course, now Heather is a raving lunatic."

The Lombardos had forbidden Heather to date Jackson again. It was the final blow for Heather, who had had to miss a month of school, and then had to wear a neck brace for another two months. A neck brace didn't really go with Heather's clothes, especially the red velvet dress she'd planned to wear to the Holiday Dance. She also had a red scar on her forehead which the doctor hoped would fade out over time, but Heather complained it was all people looked at when she talked to them. No one else had asked her out, and even though I told her it was probably because they were afraid Jackson would kill them, Heather believed it was because her looks were ruined.

I have to admit, I liked Heather better this way. I don't mean scarred up and in a neck brace. Humble. Off-balance. More like a regular girl. Sometimes when Mike and I worked at their house, she'd come in and talk to me. Once she even tried to help us work on the script, but Mike wouldn't allow it. "No ditzes," he said.

"I'm not a ditz. Besides, you told me this movie was *about* a ditz. I could help you. How do you two geniuses know how a ditz thinks?"

"Ditzes don't think," Mike said, and that was the end of it. He was very unforgiving about his sister.

Meanwhile, my social standing seemed to have risen a little bit due to all the publicity surrounding the accident. I guess it was a glamorous thing to some of the kids. They kept wanting me to talk about it. I'd say, "It's great. First you think you're going to die. Then people are crying and screaming and bleeding all over the place. Then you puke on your shoes and the police tell you you're lucky. Great way to spend a Saturday night."

It was odd; I was almost *popular*. Within a week two different guys had asked me out. Both of them, however, had "Alex Lieberman" stamped all over them. I was no longer quite so stupid as the day I decided it was better to go out with anyone than no one. No one is far better than an Alex Lieberman.

But then the week before the Holiday Dance Jeffrey Wyse walked up to me in the library and asked if I'd go with him. Jeffrey Wyse is definitely *not* an Alex Lieberman. He's smart, at least in math, which is the only class I've ever had with him, and he's treasurer of the sophomore class, which means people generally like him and know he can add. He's also reasonably nice-looking, although he doesn't smile much.

There was no good reason not to go to the dance with him, so I accepted. Mom was elated. It seemed she knew his mother as an avid reader who hung out at the library all the time, so she figured he *must* be perfect. We shopped for a dress — I thought I looked ridiculous in every single one of those satin and velvet things with bows — and found a sort of plain but slinky green dress that made me feel very grown-up, especially with Mom's long gold chain looped around my neck several times.

When I told Mike about going to the Holiday Dance, he didn't say much. "That's nice. Have fun." I expected him to be a little put out about it, I guess. The very next day he tells me *he's* going to the Junior High Holiday Dance too, with a girl named Becky.

"Who's Becky? I've never heard you mention anyone named Becky before," I said.

"I've never heard you mention this Jeffrey guy either," he countered.

I was a little confused. "Well, it's nice we're both meeting some new people."

"Isn't it?" he said snottily.

"Jeffrey is quite smart; he's class treasurer."

Mike had a smirk on his face. "Well, Becky's no rocket scientist, but she sure is cute!"

I could feel my face turning bright red as anger washed over me. "Is that all that's important to you, Mike Lombardo? Her looks? You don't even care if she's stupid?"

"I didn't say she was stupid. Look who's talking! You're the one who thought Action Jackson was so gorgeous you couldn't turn down a chance to ride in the same car with him!"

I didn't dare answer that remark, close as it was to the truth. What did I care who Mike went out with anyway?

Since the Junior High Holiday Dance was the night before the High School dance, I kept a surreptitious watch out the living room window to see how Mike looked when he left his house. I was shocked. His father had to drive him, of course, but when he walked out to the car, he looked so much older to me. He was wearing a new suit and his hair was moussed up over his face like one of the guys on *Beverly Hills 90210*. I tried to think he looked silly, but I knew it wasn't true. He looked very cute. The thought flashed through my mind that old Becky was very lucky.

The following evening Jeffrey came to the door to pick me up while his dad waited in the car. He looked pretty nice, and I could tell he thought I did too. Mom and Dad were beaming in a most embarrassing way. It wasn't exactly a bad evening, but it was very long. We danced for a while and sat at a table with his friend Conor and Conor's girlfriend, Kristy, two other smart, quiet kids. Once Kristy and I ended up in the girls' restroom at the same time.

"Jeffrey really likes you. I didn't think he'd ever get up the nerve to ask you out," Kristy said.

"You mean because he's shy?" I asked.

"People think he's shy, but that's not what it is. He's almost, I shouldn't say this, but he's even kind of conceited, I think, about how smart he is and all. So I think he couldn't stand the idea that you might say no to him. He's not used to people saying no to him."

"You don't like him too much?"

Kristy sighed. "He's okay. The thing is, he and

Conor are supposed to be best friends, but Jeffrey just tells Conor what to do all the time and Conor does it, even if he doesn't really want to, and it makes me mad."

It didn't take long for me to see just what Kristy meant.

At ten P.M. Jeffrey announced, "It's time for us to walk on down to Peaches. I've made reservations; they have fabulous appetizers and desserts."

Conor stood up immediately and waited for Kristy. We looked at each other, surprised.

"Don't worry. My dad will pick us up there at eleven-thirty," Jeffrey replied to my concerned look.

Peaches was a fancy restaurant about two blocks from the school. I'd never been there, and it did sound like a great thing to do; I was getting a little tired of dancing under crepe paper streamers, and I didn't mind missing the crowning of the king and queen. My parents might not be too happy about me walking around late at night, but I reasoned that there were four of us and the distance was not far. "Sounds like fun," I said.

"Well, Jeffrey, I wish you'd told us earlier," Kristy said. "Conor, did you know about this?"

Conor looked sheepish. "No, but don't you want to go?"

"You know how my parents are about knowing where I am every second. If I'd had a chance to discuss it with them, they'd probably say yes, but if

I call them now, they might just say they'll come and get me."

"Well then, don't call them," Jeffrey directed.

Kristy continued to look at Conor. "Besides, I'm wearing high heels, which aren't all that comfortable. Walking two blocks may not seem like much to you, but I've already been dancing in these shoes for two hours . . ."

"Kristy, the plans are made!" Jeffrey interrupted.

"Well, I didn't make them, and neither did Conor!" Kristy was angry and I didn't blame her.

"Fine! Conor you stay here with your girlfriend. We're going to Peaches."

I could tell that Conor was torn. He turned to Kristy. "Could you take your shoes off and walk barefoot?"

"In December? Are you crazy?"

"Decision's made," Jeffrey said. "Have a good time, you two." He propelled me toward the coatroom, and in a moment we were on the sidewalk.

I could see why he wanted his friends along. Left alone, he didn't have much to say, and I couldn't get over the way he'd acted toward Kristy, though I didn't bring it up. We talked about math for a minute and a half, then I asked him if he liked being on the Student Council, and he said yes. When he did speak he addressed my coat lapels. Never have two blocks seemed longer.

At least at Peaches looking at the menu and

eating gave us something to do, but when at last Mr. Wyse showed up to drive us home, I felt a wave of relief. Jeffrey was not Alex Lieberman, but he wasn't much fun either.

During the Christmas holidays he called and asked me to go to a movie with him. I didn't much want to go, but I guess I was glad he'd called. Even though I didn't like him much, he seemed to like me. It's funny how that can make a guy seem cooler than he is. So I said I'd go. Then I found out our family was supposed to go to the Lombardos' that evening for dinner.

Even though the first dinner party with the Lombardos had been a real disaster, our parents had gotten to know each other much better since then, and I figured they had enough to talk about now without embarrassing their children. And the Lombardos' house was decorated beautifully for Christmas. Just as Mom had suspected, a fifteen-foot tree filled the front bay window and, with her renewed energy, Mrs. Lombardo had draped pine boughs and holly branches throughout the house.

Besides, Mike and I hadn't had a chance to talk since the dances, and I was eager to hear how things had gone with Becky, and maybe to elaborate a little bit on the trip to Peaches. But now I'd made a date with Jeffrey Wyse, whom I didn't even like, and I'd have to miss the dinner.

The second date was even more boring than the

first. I'd thought up a list of topics beforehand, for use in an emergency: basketball, books he'd read, movies he'd liked, favorite teachers. I even thought I'd ask him who he was for in the next presidential election, figuring that would probably keep him talking for quite a while. Wrong. He answered my questions as though they were a true-false test. By the time we walked into the theater, I'd given up completely.

I knew it was going to be hard to put a good face on this dating of Jeffrey Wyse, so I decided that if Mike asked me, I'd just be honest. The next time we got together to work on the script, I took the bull by the horns.

"So," I said, "how was your date with Becky?"

"Great!" He had a big smile on his face. "She had on a knockout dress. We had a blast."

I felt like all the air had gone out of my balloon. "Are you going to ask her out again?" I asked brightly, my smile trying to match his.

Mike shrugged. "I don't know. Maybe if there's another dance. I don't think I could keep my mind on a movie if she was sitting next to me."

Oh, gag me. I couldn't believe this drivel from Mike!

"So I guess you liked Jeffrey a lot. You went out with him again," Mike said.

No sense in being entirely honest, under the circumstances. "Yes," I said with an enormous smile.

"He made reservations at Peaches after the dance. Who can say no to a guy like that?"

Mike and I sat there grinning at each other for a ridiculous amount of time, then finally got down to work without another word about our wonderful dates.

Chapter Eighteen

For the purposes of the presentation, Mike read the part of HALICE, and I read my part, Vicki. We'd decided on the name Vicki because we didn't know anyone by that name. Mike had lobbied for Heather, but I refused to go along with it. Once I accidentally wrote down Becky, but Mike ignored it, thank goodness.

Jennifer Wolodny sat in a chair in the corner of our living room, arms and legs crossed, looking skeptical.

Mike began to read in a syrupy voice.

HALICE

Hello, Vicki. I am HALICE, your Series 9000 Highly Advertised, Lovely, Insipid Computer with Emotions. I'm a gift to you from your beloved parents and I am perfect. (Sings): Happy birthday to you, happy birthday to you, happy birthday dear Vicki, happy birthday to you.

VICKI

Oh, HALICE, I love you.

HALICE

I know, Vicki.

VICKI

You don't know how long I've wished for a Series 9000 computer!

HALICE

Well, actually, I do know, Vicki. Remember, HALICE knows everything. Or at least HALICE knows as much as you know. I've been programmed to be just like you, Vicki, so that we can be best friends.

VICKI

A best friend at last! And you're so beautiful!

HALICE

Of course I am, Vicki. I'm beautiful because you're beautiful.

VICKI

Oooh! Would you mind if I, like, brushed your hair . . . and, like, . . . put it in a French braid?

HALICE

That would be lovely, Vicki. Could I, like, brush your hair and, like, put it in a French braid too?

104

VICKI [*Close to tears*]

Oh, HALICE, no one has ever wanted to French braid my hair before. I might cry!

HALICE

Oh, Vicki, please don't cry. Remember, I'm, like, your best friend and if you cry, I have to cry too. And if my circuit boards get wet, your daddy will have to take me to the repair shop. [*Starts to cry too.*] And I *hate* the repair shop! Those men have such big, rough hands, and the way they pull my wires . . .

"Wait a minute," Jennifer interrupted. "You mean, I have to French braid your hair wearing a pair of oven mitts and without being able to see what I'm doing?"

I looked at Mike; I hadn't thought about that problem.

"We wouldn't have to film what you were actually doing," Mike decided. "As long as it appears that you're braiding her hair, it'll look fine."

Jennifer didn't look convinced. "Are you going to put my name on the screen for all the world to see?"

I was a little hurt. "Well, not if you don't want us to. Really, Jennifer, you don't have to do it at all if you hate it so much."

105

"I didn't say that. It's kind of funny actually. I mean, I like the idea of the smart dumb computer. Skip to a really funny part."

I sighed. "How about the part where they're talking about Vicki's boyfriend?" I said to Mike. We flipped ahead in the script.

HALICE

Good morning, Vicki. I want to thank you again for letting me meet Billy last night. He's very cute, just like you said he was.

VICKI

Isn't he, HALICE? You know, he's, like, the captain of the football team, the baseball team, the soccer team, the volleyball team, and the golf team.

HALICE

I thought only presidents played golf, Vicki. Is Billy going to be a president someday?

VICKI

Not if he marries me, he isn't! I don't want to live in that big drafty house where they let the tourists walk around and look at the dishes you eat your dinner off of. I just want him to make a lot of money!

HALICE

What do you think Billy will be when ~rows up, Vicki?

VICKI

Well, maybe he'll be a famous football player, or a famous baseball player, or maybe he'll just, like, find some pirate treasure that was hidden on a beach hundreds of years ago, and, like, I'll get to keep all the diamonds, but we'll put everything else into blue-chip stocks and buy, like, a Tudor mansion in Brookline.

HALICE

That would be very nice, Vicki. Can I ask you a question?

VICKI

Of course you can, HALICE. You're my best friend.

HALICE

Do best friends come along when you get married, Vicki?

VICKI

Oh, I don't know. Usually they don't, HALICE, but since you're a computer, you probably could, if Billy said you could.

HALICE

Oh, I don't think Billy would mind, Vicki.

VICKI

I don't think he would either. [*Thinking it over*] Why do you think he wouldn't mind?

HALICE

Well, Vicki, Billy and I became friends last night. Do you remember when you went to the bathroom, Vicki? I had a nice talk with Billy.

VICKI

Oh, really? I suppose you talked mostly about me, didn't you?

HALICE

Actually, Vicki, Billy wanted to talk about me. You know, Vicki, Billy likes blondes.

VICKI

Of course I know he likes blondes. I'm a blonde, aren't I?

HALICE

Yes, you are, Vicki. And so am I.

VICKI [*Thinking it over*]

Maybe you won't come with me when I get married after all.

HALICE

Billy might be very disappointed, Vicki. Billy says my lips are very soft.

VICKI

What? You're lying! Billy wouldn't kiss a computer! Your lips are plastic!

HALICE

Some men like plastic, Vicki. And I'm not just *any* old computer, Vicki. I'm a Series 9000 computer and I am ex- like you.

108

Jennifer Wolodny was actually laughing. "It's good, it's good. I like it. Of course, I've seen the dumb movie before. I'm not sure it'll be as funny to people who haven't seen the movie."

"First of all, the movie isn't dumb, it's camp," Mike explained impatiently. "Secondly, I think it does work without the movie. I read it to Heather and even *she* thought it was funny."

"So what else happens?" Jennifer asked.

"Well, that's sort of the beginning of the end," Mike said. "They start fighting and Vicki realizes that HALICE has begun to take over her whole world. Vicki's parents like HALICE more than they like Vicki, her teachers and even her dog prefer HALICE. So finally, in a mad rage Vicki rips the computer apart. HALICE keeps talking for a while, running down more and more, and finally she gurgles to a stop . . ."

"Then —" I interrupted, wanting to tell my own punch line, "Vicki turns to the camera with this weird smile on her face and says, 'Hello, I'm VICKI, your Series 9000 computer, and I'm perfect!'"

Jennifer applauded. I knew I must be beaming. I'd never had anything I'd written publicly appreciated before. It was a truly great feeling.

"Okay," she said. "I'm in. My acting debut will be as a computer ripped to shreds by a cheerleader."

"Listen, you two sign the contracts," Mike said. "I told my mom I'd be home by now to help her clean the house. Thanks to your mom we've started a new regimen. We all have to help with house chores so she can have time for herself. She's taking classes, you know. My mother, the phobic turned psychologist." He said it as though it bugged him, but I knew good and well that the whole family was relieved at the way Mrs. Lombardo had changed.

After Mike left, Jennifer said, "Well, I have to admit, he's a cute kid, especially now that he's getting a little taller. Still, you spend an awful lot of time with him."

"Please. Let's not start this again," I begged.

"Are you still going out with Jeffrey Wyse?"

"I don't think so. He called me again last week, but I said I had too much homework to do. I don't think he'll call again. I've been told he doesn't like to be turned down."

"What's wrong with you? Don't you like him? Jeez, he gets straight As!"

"Does he?"

"He's treasurer of the sophomore class!"

"Great. I'll call him when I can't balance my checkbook."

"Who would you *rather* be going out with?"

I thought about that question. "Nobody, I guess. I just don't think dating is all that much fun. You either get mauled or bored to death."

"You know this from your vast experience with
'sume."

"Sue me. I can't think of anybody I'd really *like* to go out with."

"Except the kid across the street. You go out with him all the time."

"We go to the movies. We don't 'go out.' "

"I call that going out. You went to the movies with Jeffrey Wyse and you called it going out."

"No, I called that wasting my time."

Jennifer shook her head. "I don't get it. You'd rather be making these goofy movies with a child than dating a high school guy. A lot of girls would be thrilled to go out with Jeffrey. You're demented."

Maybe she was right. I thought about last year, how I never spoke to anyone and just came home alone and read books. I didn't want to return to that life anymore. Now that I had a few friends, a small social life, it was more fun going to school. I didn't want to be invisible again.

"What's wrong with Jeffrey anyway?" Jennifer continued. "I think he's cute in a serious sort of way."

"Maybe you're right," I conceded. "Maybe I'll call him. It wouldn't hurt to go to the movies with him."

Jennifer made a disgusted face. "Don't do him any favors."

Chapter Nineteen

We spent all of February and March shooting the movie. Mike was a tough director and Jennifer and I couldn't help getting frustrated sometimes.

"You're losing the voice, Jennifer," he'd say. "Justine, talk to HALICE, not the camera, remember? Let's try it again."

We shot the same scenes over and over, until we were so sick of the whole thing, we wanted to quit, but Mike never wavered. "This is not just a joke, you know. We'll do it until we get it right."

"Who does this kid think he is, Steven Spielberg?" Jennifer exploded one day while Mike was out of the room. "Does he think he's going to win an Academy Award with this dumb movie?"

I had to admit Mike was getting on my nerves too, but I stood up for him anyway. "He's a perfectionist. He's always wanted to make a movie and he just wants to do it right."

"Right, wrong. What's the difference? Who's ever going to see this epic anyway?"

It was a question that had occurred to me too. I decided to put it to Mike while we were walking home one afternoon. "Do you have any plans for showing this film once it's finished? I mean, it's nice just to do it, but, I don't know, what's the point of making a movie that nobody is going to see?"

"I thought of that," Mike said. "That's why I went to the local cable station last week and talked to the manager."

"You did? Why didn't you tell me?"

"Because you'd have wanted to come along, and I figured if he was going to laugh at me, I'd just as soon not have an audience."

"He didn't laugh, did he?"

Mike smiled. "Nope. He said he'd be happy to look at a rough cut once I've started editing it. They *like* to run local stuff; he was actually *pleased* I'd come in. Chances are, unless he thinks it's really idiotic, he'll show it."

"Wow. Everybody in town could see it." Suddenly I was having second thoughts. What would the kids at school think? Everybody would know how much time I spent with an eighth grader. What if people thought the movie was totally stupid?

"You don't seem all that thrilled," Mike said, picking up my anxiety.

"No, it'll be great. Just, what if people don't like it?"

"Of course people won't like it. *Some* people won't. Some people will. If you're going to be an artist, you have to face the fact that not everybody is going to appreciate your work. That's no reason not to do it."

I nodded thoughtfully.

"You're not worried about *people*. You're worried about *Jeffrey*, aren't you? You're afraid he'll think it's weird, that maybe he shouldn't be dating someone who makes movies about talking computers."

While not right on the money, this guess was uncomfortably close to the truth, so of course I denied it vehemently. "Jeffrey knows about the movie already. Besides, I don't care what anybody thinks."

I had dated Jeffrey four or five more times. He seemed glad to go out with me, but not eager to escalate the romance, which was fine with me. People talked about us as though we were a couple, which made high school life easier, but I didn't actually have to spend all that much time with him. Usually I saw him for a few minutes before and after school, but we had different lunch periods, so we weren't forced to eat together.

To tell you the truth, I wasn't that crazy about the guy. He just had no sense of humor. He was fine if you needed help with a math problem or something, but he didn't seem to know how to have fun. The last time we'd gone out, he walked me to the door afterward, and I could tell he thought it was about time he kissed me. After all, we'd dated off and on for three months, and anybody else would be more romantically advanced by that time, but the truth is, neither of us cared about it much. So we had an obligatory kiss or two and then I felt really depressed.

"I've been wanting to do that," he said unconvincingly.

"Me too," I lied.

After that he obviously wanted to go home, so he did that too, without another word. Was dating always going to be this excruciating?

Of course, I didn't *have* to date Jeffrey, but it was easy in a way. Pretending to like each other in front of other kids was actually more fun than being on a date alone. I hated to admit it, but I think I was beginning to like fitting in.

And, of course, Mike had a whole new social life too. Since we'd been using our Saturday and Sunday afternoons to shoot our movie, Mike and I hadn't had time to go into Cambridge much. So he'd started taking Becky to the early evening shows. As a matter of fact, the one time I talked Jeffrey into going to a foreign film, Truffaut's *Jules and Jim,* which he yawned all the way through, we ran into Mike and Becky in the lobby.

She was very small and pretty. A little too giggly, I thought, but then I was able to identify my basic emotion as jealousy, so I tried to give her the benefit of the doubt. As they walked away down the street, she grabbed Mike's arm and laughed. Jeez, I thought, she acts twenty-one.

Not that I was jealous that Mike had a date, I told myself. Just that he was having so much fun with her, and I was stuck with a stick-in-the-mud. Oh, I did my share of laughing and eye-rolling while we stood on the sidewalk making introductions too, but it was strictly acting, my best performance.

It was Becky I was thinking about that afternoon as Mike and I walked along.

"Does she know about the movie?" I asked him.

He was startled. "Who?"

"Becky."

He blushed slightly. "Sure. We've talked about it. She likes to . . . talk about . . . anything."

All I had to do was mention her name and he was flustered. I gave him a long look, but now he was studying the sidewalk as though there were gold coins to be found there.

"Do you really like Becky?" I kept making myself say her name.

"Yeah. She's a good kid. And she likes me."

"I asked if you like her, not whether she likes you."

"I said, yes, I do like her. Can't you tell?"

A feeling of total fury came over me, from out of nowhere, and I threw my books from one arm to the other, just to be making a large, decisive movement, but instead I dropped every one of them on the ground.

"Damn," I said and got down on my knees to pick them up.

Mike looked at me in surprise when I swore, which I hardly ever did, and got down to help me pick the stuff up.

"What's wrong?" he asked.

"I just dropped all this stuff! I've got so damn much homework tonight." When we stood up I tried to take the books back that Mike had picked up.

"I'll carry these," he said. "I've only got one book." For some reason I suddenly remembered the night of the accident and how Mike sat on the table next to me and held my hand. There were tears just barely restrained inside my eyes. I blinked and turned aside so Mike couldn't see them. What in the world were they there for?

"You look funny. Are you feeling all right?"

"No, actually, I think I'm getting sick." With every word Mike said to me, I felt worse. I felt like his voice had gotten inside of me and was banging into everything. I even felt sick in my stomach. But it wasn't the flu. I felt . . . hurt. My whole body just felt hurt.

Mike walked me to the Pizza Pan and called his mother, who promised to come right out and pick us up. While he called, I went into the bathroom and let the tears out. I hated cute little Becky and I hated smart old Jeffrey and I hated the whole state of Massachusetts.

Chapter Twenty

I didn't see as much of Mike the next few months. He was editing the movie by himself, so he was busy. Once I went over to see how it was coming, but he seemed edgy when I was around, like he was afraid I'd give him some dumb advice or something.

The movie opened with the theme music from *2001*, the heavy dramatic music that comes on when the monkeys are dancing around the stone, then, when the titles came on, the music changed to the theme from the *My Little Pony* cartoon. It was very funny, but Mike didn't laugh along with me. He just stared into the editing machine Dad had borrowed for him from the University.

"I really look ridiculous in that blonde wig," I commented, just to have something to say.

"You're supposed to look ridiculous, remember?" he said scornfully.

"I know, but now that I know the whole town's going to see me . . ."

"All of a sudden you're a prima donna! All of a sudden nothing's right!"

"I didn't say that!"

"I can't change things at the last minute, you know." I guess he was really nervous, so I decided to stay out of his way. It was hard to talk to him, and that made me feel lonely.

Anyway, he was doing a great job without any help; he'd already shown a rough cut to the cable station manager and it was O.K.'ed for airing beginning on May 3, so he had to finish it quickly.

I still went out with Jeffrey once in a while. We'd dropped the kissing after a few more tries; we just didn't feel that way about each other. I felt more comfortable around him, like he was a friend, even though we never had much to talk about. I guess I mostly kept going out with him because he kept asking me and I didn't have much else to do.

Of course Mom started referring to him as my "boyfriend," and one time she said, "I hope you and Jeffrey aren't getting too serious."

I said, "You don't get it, Mom. Jeffrey just *is* serious."

She gave me a look. "He's not putting pressure on you, is he? Don't let him talk you into anything you're not ready for."

I had to laugh. The only thing Jeffrey pressured me about was not going to any more foreign films. Still, I hated to tell her the truth: that we didn't even like each other all that much; we were just hanging on until something better came along.

Mike and I stopped meeting after school. For one thing, somebody had asked Jeffrey if I was dating an eighth grader, and he kept wanting to know who the "little germ" was. But it was really Mike who stopped coming to meet me, not the other way around. Since the day I dropped my books near the Pizza Pan, Mike acted weird. Like the time I said, "*The 400 Blows* is in the Square this weekend. Are you and Becky going to see it?"

He practically took my head off. "Not everyone in the world loves old Truffaut movies, Justine. I suppose you're going with the Wise-Guy?"

"Actually, no. He doesn't like foreign films." I had hoped that Becky wouldn't like them either, and maybe Mike and I could go together, like old times, but that notion didn't seem to occur to him.

"We're not going to the movies at all," he scowled. "Becky says we see too many movies. There's this dance at the school."

"Do you like dances?" It was a stupid question, but it had gotten hard to think of something to say.

"I can't even dance! Why would I like dances?"

"I bet a lot of guys in the eighth grade don't dance. I could teach you if you want, not that I'm so great, but it's fun to . . ."

He backed away from me as if I had suddenly

121

begun to smell. "Who do you think you are, my big sister?"

"No. I just . . ."

He pulled out ahead and stomped on down the sidewalk. Finally he slowed up and waited for me. "Sorry. Guess I'm in a crummy mood," he said. All the way home I kept trying to think of something nice to say to him. I hated seeing him looking so unhappy, but how could I help him feel better if I didn't know why he was upset? I had this urge to touch him, to sort of comfort him, but I couldn't possibly have done that. Even if he didn't punch me in the face, I'd be making a fool of myself.

*   *   *

Spring came early that year. It was so warm that Jennifer, who never walked anywhere if she could help it, began walking partway home with me after school.

"So, is the kid going to get it finished in time?" she asked in late April. "He's only got two more weeks."

"I know. I don't dare ask him, he's gotten so moody lately."

"I hope he's not going to let puberty disrupt our movie!" Now that the airing was imminent, Jennifer had gotten very possessive about the film.

"He'll get it done. Are you kidding? He's wanted to do this all his life."

"His short life."

"Jennifer, I wish you'd get off his back. He's two years, no, a year and a half, younger than us. This does not make him an alien being."

"Combined with his male gender, it certainly does."

I gave up. "Mom's putting together a big party for May third. The Lombardos are all coming and she's going to invite you and your parents . . ."

"Who else?"

"I don't know. Maybe a few kids from school." I suddenly had a thought; what if Becky was coming? "I guess I'll ask Jeffrey to come."

"Good!" Jennifer smiled. "I've never actually met him, but he seems like a neat guy."

"I guess so."

"Jeez, I've never known anybody who liked their boyfriend less than you do," Jennifer complained.

"I know. It's pathetic."

"If you don't want him, you ought to pass him on to someone who does."

"Why? Do you know somebody who wants him?" I asked, surprised. Jennifer blushed. "*You* do? Why didn't you tell me?"

"What should I say? I like your boyfriend more than you do?"

"He's really not my boyfriend. We're hardly even friends. Look, I'll invite him on the third and you can meet him."

"Don't do me any favors," Jennifer crabbed, but I could tell she was excited by the idea that Jeffrey was not private property. It occurred to me that I might regret handing over my boyfriend if Mike and Becky showed up looking like poster children for lovesickness, but I was tired of pretending I had some kind of relationship with a guy who bored me silly.

Chapter Twenty-one

Our living room was starting to fill up with people, everybody but Mike. The Lombardos and the Wolodnys had the comfortable seats, but Mom had brought in kitchen chairs and pillows from all over the house for the kids to sit on. Heather came with her new boyfriend, Eric, also handsome, but less conceited than Jackson, who had finally given up on Heather and was now going steady with a teenage model.

Jeffrey was there right on time, of course, and Conor and Kristy came along too. Then a couple of girls from my English class I'd gotten to know recently showed up. Jennifer was mad I'd invited other females because she felt I'd promised Jeffrey to her, but I mentioned that any final decision on the matter really ought to be up to him. I did give her a great buildup, though, when I introduced them, and the next time I checked, sure enough, they were huddled together on two chairs, avidly discussing some serious issue.

The movie was supposed to start at 8 o'clock, but it was 7:50 and Mike still wasn't there. Mom had been having me run around getting people drinks and putting out snacks, but I finally managed to get Heather alone for a minute and ask nonchalantly, "So, I guess Mike walked over to get Becky, huh?"

Heather looked surprised. "I don't think so. He hasn't gone out with her in a long time. When I left the house he was standing in front of the bathroom mirror swearing at his hair. I said, 'You're only going across the street, not to the senior prom.' He slammed the door in my face." She turned back to Eric. "And they say girls are vain."

Just as the announcer came on to explain that the film we were about to see was made by local students, Mike slipped quietly in the door. I guess I hadn't seen much of him lately. He looked terrific, tall and thin. Tall? When had he gotten so tall? He was wearing a chambray shirt and jeans, and his hair, his lovely hair, was combed so that it fell softly over his forehead. Just as I caught his eye, he ran his hand through it as though he was exasperated and just wanted to push it away. Just seeing him do that made my cheeks flame up and I looked away from him, embarrassed. I kept saying to myself, It's just Mike, what's the matter with you?

But the movie was starting and everyone got very

126

quiet. For about half a minute there was no sound in the room, and just as I was starting to get nervous — the theme music was playing, weren't they getting it? — everybody started to laugh. And they kept laughing, through the entire twenty minutes.

When it was over everybody started to whoop and applaud and tell us how great it was. Mom and Dad came over to give me a hug and to shake Mike's hand. The announcer was back on talking about giving credit to our youth instead of concentrating on the problem kids, and how we had written and filmed and edited the whole thing ourselves with no adult help.

I couldn't help feeling very proud of myself and of Mike and even of Jennifer. We'd really done a pretty amazing thing. And all these people seemed to know it. It was great to feel so appreciated.

Mom brought out the ice cream then and sundae toppings, and everybody made themselves a big dish before there was a cry to rewind the tape and watch the movie again. But for some reason I just didn't want to see it again with this crowd of admirers. I felt so full and happy, it was kind of scary, I think, and I just wanted to be alone for a minute. With all the noise in the house it was easy to slip out the front door without being seen.

There, sitting on the front porch steps, was Mike.

"What are you doing out here?" I asked, my heart picking up its beat. When had I last had a

127

good talk with him? Suddenly I missed him terribly.

"I could ask you the same thing," he shot back.

"I just needed a breather. I felt like if I smiled anymore, my face would break open."

"I know. Want to take a walk?"

"Sure," I said, as though we were just the same as always, on our way to the movies or school. But I felt so different.

We walked very slowly and silently for about a block. I could hardly breathe; it seemed like there was a giant magnet between us and I had to force myself to stand upright so my blouse wouldn't be sucked up against Mike's shirt. When we came alongside the Bakers' garage, Mike suddenly walked over and leaned up against it, as though he was too tired to keep walking.

"We can go back if you want," Mike said.

"Why would I want to?"

He ran his hand through his hair again. "I know how you feel about being seen with a guy who's not good-looking."

I had to laugh, thinking of that old argument we'd had. "Oh, come on," I said, without thinking about it, "you know you're gorgeous." I meant it as a joke, but as soon as I said it, I realized it was true. Mike suddenly seemed very attractive to me. Very, very. Of course he'd always been perfectly nice-looking, but now — had his looks changed that much or was it just the way I felt about him that made him seem so different?

Then the magnet pulled me over until I was standing right in front of him. It happened very quickly.

Mike picked up my hands in his and pulled me near him. He didn't really have to do much pulling because I was ready to go there anyway. And then he kissed me. It was nothing at all like the kisses I'd gotten from or given to Jeffrey Wyse. This kiss made me dizzy, and I couldn't imagine how life could go on in the same way when it was over.

But then it was over, and we were standing very close together, staring at each other, blinking.

Mike, at least, had the garage to lean against for support, but I felt like I was swaying in the breeze with a decision to be made about which direction I was headed in next. All these crazy thoughts were stumbling around in my brain. This is an eighth grader! This is Mike! He's wonderful! This is the kid who hides in the bushes! I saw him get beaten up! I want to touch his hair! This is Heather's brother! Kiss me again! It was just too confusing, and I think I pulled away from him just because I wasn't sure exactly who he was.

As soon as I did, Mike stood up. "Celebratory kiss," he said hoarsely. "We did a good job." He started to walk back toward my house and I followed him.

"We did."

"Great team, huh? Let's make another one. Get down to work, kiddo. Write me another screen-play." He smiled, but it was a hard smile. We didn't say another word to each other all evening.

Chapter Twenty-two

For two weeks, Mike and I avoided each other. Meanwhile, I had to listen to Jennifer every day at lunchtime.

"Jeffrey is so great! I don't know why you didn't appreciate him. Although I must say, he wasn't that crazy about you either."

"Thanks, Jennifer. I needed to know that."

"Like you thought he was madly in love with you?"

"So, what do you talk about with him? I could never get him to say two words, unless it was about math."

"I love math! Besides, he likes to talk about railroads, and hockey and reptiles . . . did you even know he's got a pet snake?"

"I repeat: we had nothing in common."

"Well, it's a fair trade. I introduced you to Sylvia Plath and you introduced me to Jeffrey Wyse. We're even," she deduced.

When I thought of it that way, it seemed like I may even have gotten the better end of the deal.

But it didn't help me out when I was sitting alone in my room and suddenly realized I'd been staring out the window for twenty minutes, my eyes fixed on the curtains of Mike's room. You are ridiculous, I told myself. Yes, Mike has gotten better-looking over the past few months, but he's still too immature for you. As soon as you meet somebody else with soft brown hair who loves old movies and is fun to be with. . . . It wasn't working. I felt like a crazy person: all I could think about was his hand, his hair, The Kiss. It wasn't fair. I wanted to be crazy about someone who'd get a driver's license before I did.

Then Saturday afternoon, Mike called.

"Hey. You wanna come over? The trees are all leaved out behind the house and Heather's balcony is almost like a tree house again."

I hesitated. Why was I going over? There was no movie to work on. No good reason to go. "I was writing my government report," I lied. "But maybe I could come over for a minute, just to see." It was hopeless. My mouth was no longer under my control.

"Sure, I've got some other stuff to do today too."

Two minutes later we were standing on opposite sides of Heather's balcony, like people who hardly knew each other at all.

132

"Let's make another movie," Mike finally blurted out.

"Another movie?"

"Sure, why not? The first one was fun, wasn't it? And a big success." In fact, the movie was all the kids at school talked about the week after it first aired. I had turned into a minor celebrity and I imagined Mike had as well. There had even been an article in the local newspaper with both of our pictures included. But how could we make another movie together now? Everything had changed.

"I don't know, Mike. Maybe we should wait a while," I hedged.

"That's not the way it's done. You build on your successes. I had an idea. Maybe we could do a take-off on Truffaut's *Wild Child* — the kid raised by wolves."

"Maybe. I'd have to think about it."

"You don't like the idea."

"It's not that. I just feel like I need a break before I do another movie."

Mike's face tightened up like a mask. "A break from me?"

"No, that's not what I mean. Okay, maybe it is."

"Because I gave you one little kiss?"

That was *little?* "I don't know. I mean, are we still friends or what?"

"Well, if you don't know that much after all this time . . ."

"I know we *were* friends, but if you're kissing me, if we're . . . well, how can we still be friends? I feel like we can't go back to that."

"And you want to go back?" he asked, his mouth twitching.

There was part of me that wanted to run over and hug him and tell him how I really felt, but it seemed my whole body, legs, arms, tongue, everything, was tied with ropes, like I could only do and say what some giant puppeteer allowed. "It's just that I don't know . . . I don't know . . . ," I mumbled.

"Look, forget it! Jeez — one little kiss! I'll never touch you again, okay?"

Mike turned his back to me then and leaned against the railing, looking out over the back yard. I felt sick to my stomach again, only even worse than before. I *wanted* Mike to like me, to touch me, and I wanted to touch him, to apologize to him. I couldn't bear to see him so angry at me. There was nobody I liked more than Mike. How could one and a half lousy years matter that much? What was the matter with me?

I willed my muscles to unfreeze and slowly I inched closer to him, but his back was still turned. I forced my hand through the thick air, and as I did I heard a strange creaking noise. For a moment I thought it must have come from my own rusty joints, but just as my hand reached Mike's back, he turned halfway around with a look of such surprise, even fear, that I realized there was more going on in the world than a girl touching a boy.

Before I could understand what it was, the railing where Mike was leaning gave way, and he began to fall forward through the air. I think I was screaming while he fell, but not so loudly that it covered the thud of his body hitting the ground. He made a sound as though all the breath was going out of him and rolled over onto his back in a pile of leaf mulch near the side of the house.

The next thing I remember was kneeling on the ground beside him, and he wasn't moving. For a minute I just stared at him; I couldn't imagine what I should do. "Please be all right," I whispered, as though my words were magic.

Some leaves had gotten stuck in his hair, and for some reason I started to brush them out, brush his hair back out of his eyes. But as soon as my fingers felt his hair, which I'd wanted to touch so often before, a curtain of tears began to slide down my face. "I'm sorry," I kept saying over and over. "I'm so sorry."

Mike opened his eyes. "Hey, for our next movie, can I be the stuntman?"

I grabbed his hands to stop mine from shaking. "Oh, you're not dead, are you?" I started to laugh, even though I was still crying.

"I don't think so. Help me up." I helped him into a sitting position and he groaned.

"Did you hurt your back? Did you hit your head? You flew through the air!"

"With the greatest of ease. No, I think I'm okay."

"What should I do? Should I get you something? Do you want to try to stand up?"

"Not yet. There is one thing you could do for me," he said, looking more than a little embarrassed. "Comb your fingers through my hair like that again."

And I did, without saying a word. And he was looking up at me with this soft look, and I'm sure he could see me shivering.

"A fall from a balcony deserves a kiss," he said. "Lombardo's Law."

He barely got the words out of his mouth before my lips were on it. It was just like before, only better, more relaxed. When I stopped kissing him, we sat together in the leaves, holding hands.

"So, what do I get if I fall off the roof?" Mike asked.

Then we laughed for a while and tickled each other. I felt so relieved, not just because Mike was all right, but because he was Mike again and I was me, only now it was even better.

Mike put his arm around my waist. "Did you kiss Jeffrey?"

"Yeah, but it wasn't like this."

136

Mike nodded. "I kissed Becky a few times, but it was like practicing for Amateur Night, and this is like being on Broadway."

"No more pretending," I agreed.

We sat there together in the leaf mulch for a few more minutes, then got up and got moving. We realized we just had time to make it into Cambridge for *Fahrenheit 451* at the Brattle Theater, which might just give us the inspiration for our next movie.